IT'S *Not Right* FOR Wo-MAN TO BE *Alone*

THE REAL REASON YOU'RE SINGLE

KELSIE HARRIS-KNIGHT

Dedication

I dedicate this book first to God who is perfecting love in me daily. I walk this walk not out of obligation or compulsion but because of Love. You first loved me and wrote the book of my life with that love.

To my mother, one of the most significant people in my life. You have always been a motivator and a force to be reckoned with. Thank you for raising me to be strong and also a force to be reckoned with. I love and honor you for it.

To my father, I love and appreciate you.

To my Olivia, who taught me one of the greatest lessons of my life. You are my true beauty in exchange for ashes.

To Sheldon, thank you for showing me how gentle love can be.

Acknowledgments

I want to thank God. This book is an outward expression of the inward work that He personally took time to see me through. It was only God that could have pulled this out of me, and He knew I needed to begin the healing process this way. He knew it would take me over ten years to write. The journey would bring me to the place I am today and make me into the woman I am now. I am *nothing* apart from Him.

Contents

Introduction   9

Chapter 1   The Root of It All   13

Chapter 2   Broken Record   23

Chapter 3   Image Matters   31

Chapter 4   Understanding Your Trigger   35

Chapter 5   Recognizing Your Fear   43

Chapter 6   The Awakening   49

Chapter 7   Clarity in Chaos   73

Chapter 8   My First Love   85

Chapter 9   Take Care of You   95

Chapter 10 The Shift   109

Chapter 11 Go After Boaz!   117

Changing Direction: Breaking Unhealthy Relationship Patterns   **121**
An Interactive Workbook

Session 1: The Root of It All   123

Session 2: Scripts and Schemas   129

Session 3: Broken Record   135

Session 4: Image Matters   139

Session 5: Understanding Your Triggers   143

Session 6: Chaos in Clarity   147

Session 7: Taking Care of You   149

Introduction

All of creation began with a pattern. When God created us, He had a specific pattern for us—that pattern was His image. And God said, *"Let Us make man in Our image, according to Our likeness"* (Genesis 1:26). We are so precious to God that He wanted us shaped and formed in His righteousness and holiness. We were to be sagacious in our mind, possess holiness in our heart, and righteousness was to govern our actions. These attributes were to order our life in such a way that it compels us to be effective and possess this earth.

At one point, we understood this pattern; we understood authority, we understood our potential, and we understood all the limitlessness of our abilities. Our relationship with God was not schismatic; it was communal. There was nothing hidden about God and nothing hidden about man. God's intended pattern was perfect and functional until sin entered.

In the book of Genesis, when man sinned, God's intended pattern became distorted, thereby causing him to no longer behold himself in God's image. When the relationship between man and God is ruptured, man's understanding of self is not discernible. There is no longer a coherent objective; man now independently searches to understand who he is through his own exertions and abilities. God's intended pattern was skewed through man's own efforts, and man became deficient, inadequate, and ineffective apart from Him.

God said to Jeremiah, *"Before I formed you in the womb I knew you; before you were born I sanctified you; I ordained you a prophet to the nations"* (Jeremiah 1:5). "Formed" is the Hebrew word *yatsar*, meaning God in creative activity molded, fashioned, and determined him. The word "knew" is the Hebrew word *yada*, which means to intimately and personally have knowledge of. Within this context, God speaks to Jeremiah of the intimate, creative activity that took place when He personally formed and determined him to be a prophet to the nations. God spoke to Jeremiah from a place of surety; Jeremiah, in turn, responded to God from a place deficiency. *"Ah, Lord God! Behold, I cannot speak, for I am a youth"* (Jeremiah 1:6). Jeremiah couldn't see what God saw.

A pattern is a repetitious, consistent sequence of behaviors that manifest itself the same way every time. In order for us to live out God's pattern for our life, we must collaboratively work in relationship with Him. It is through the development of our personal relationship with God that we are able to form healthy, functional relationships with others.

In the overall scheme of life, no relationship you will ever form will have the capacity to function succinctly outside of your own personal relationship with God. It is through relationship with God that we come to a revelation of who we are and who He created us to be. Your knowledge of self will govern every decision you will ever make in the span of your lifetime. Every decision you make will ultimately yield a consequence that will direct the course of your life. A consequence is simply something that is produced after following a set of decisions. It is the end result of your choices.

What does this have to do with your relationships, specifically with the opposite sex? If you were to reflect on all of your past relationships and be truthful with yourself, you would notice that there are certain patterns your relationships have a tendency to follow. Whether successful or catastrophic, your relationships speak volumes to your ability to relate to the opposite sex. For most of us, the vulnerability that comes along with being emotionally intimate with another person is terrifying.

What is even more terrifying is that we have absolutely no knowledge that this fear exists.

Our bookshelves are teeming with books and magazines about being happy and single and waiting for that ideal mate. It's great to have these resources, but how is it that you can hardly find resources that confront the issue of why we are single in the first place? As Christians, we have convinced ourselves that the only reason we are single is because we are simply *waiting on God*. Do not misunderstand me when I say this, because I completely and adamantly believe in divine delay and developing patience in the area of waiting for the man God has for you. But truth be told, our delay is often because we are unable to function in a relationship. If that ideal mate were to enter our life, the relationship would not last; we would be unable to sustain it simply because we overlook, ignore, or we simply rationalize our ineffective patterns that make us unsuccessful in this area of our lives.

When the Lord placed this book on my heart, I wondered, *Lord, how could I possibly help anyone in the area of relationships? My relationship history sucked! What could I possibly tell others?* The Lord showed me that many people have been broken in relationships, and the problem is that they are caught in a cycle in which they continually stay stuck in the same type of relationship. They are stuck in a pattern of bad decisions and bad actions.

Years ago, the Lord spoke to me in a dream. In the dream, the Lord warned me and said, "You have to pay attention to your patterns, because if you don't you will never be any good to the kingdom." I knew right then that He was talking mainly about the area in my life I struggled the most—my relationships with the opposite sex. Whereas what God spoke to me can be utilized in so many other areas, at that time it ministered with specific emphasis on my relationship patterns. I would later find out that it was minimally about the process of finding a good mate and everything to do with my self-worth, my understanding of who I am, and most of all who He created me to be.

* * *

This book is not written to help you find a mate but, in actuality, to help you find you! In reading this, my hope and prayer is to help you divulge every broken place in your mind and heart that continually lands you in the pit of broken relationships. *You* are the reason you cannot maintain a healthy relationship! That's right, I said it!

Chapter 1

The Root of It All

Ah, Lord God! Behold, I cannot speak, for I am a youth (Jeremiah 1:6).

At the age of twenty-one, I received a call that would forever change my life. It was my sister, sounding frantic, saying, "Kelsie, Melissa is in the hospital, and I don't think she is going to make it." There is always something significant about the last time you see a person. Something about that memory stands out, at least for me it did. That memory felt like love. The moment that you realize you meant something to someone, that you mattered to their life, negates all the questions and apprehensions you had about them before, and it solidifies, or better yet validates, your love for them. For me, it was the moment in the bus station when, for the first time in our friendship, Melissa and I hugged, and she said to me, "I'll see you soon." At that moment, I felt loved. That was the last time I saw her alive. Melissa was my best friend from high school. By best friend, I mean really my only friend.

I've always felt like love evades me. It has always been the thing I sought after and have been chasing. It is outside of me and always around me, but never within me. I would love to get all holy with you and say it wasn't until I found God that love finally was with me, but it's not that easy. In the spiritual sense, Love was living in me, but understanding how to embrace something that had always seemed so distant and unattainable is a whole other story. People preach love, but many don't truly walk in it or know how to really love. Self-love is the biggest paradox; it's this inward concept that people seek to find outwardly. What I mean is that people start spending time with themselves, dressing up, or doing activities or hobbies they love, defending themselves, standing up for themselves, and speaking up against things that harm them, but that's all outward.

My biggest enemy is the one that wakes me up at three o'clock in the morning, reminding me of all the pain and past hurt. The deep feelings of loneliness and regret. The constant flashbacks of those who have left—and those who are still here but add to the pain. The self-loathing, the anxiety of past mistakes, and the fear of the mistakes to come. I've experienced glimpses of love but not the tenure of love. I've been searching after it and seeking it, but it's evaded me.

God in His infinite knowledge and wisdom knows all things, but He imparts His plans for your life in pieces. He has a tendency to leave certain details out. I have come to understand that, in all things, God creates or allows a circumstance in such a way that we are to seek Him in order to figure it out. His plan is not always easily spelled out, and the path is never obvious.

The more I come to discover God for myself, the more questions I have. The biggest question throughout my journey has always been, *Why did You allow me to go through this; wasn't there an easier way?* For years, I thought I never had a chance from the beginning. I thought the odds were stacked against me before I was old enough to know better, and by the time I was old enough to do better, the damage was done. I was already stuck in patterns that were unhealthy and toxic.

My story began in Guyana, South America. I was born and lived there until the age of seven. The first memory I have is sitting on the outside stairwell of my grandmother's house, watching a plane fly above my head. I sat there gazing at the plane and wondering if that was the plane my parents were on. When I was about two years old, my parents immigrated to the United States. The decision was made that my siblings and I would stay with my grandparents until we were able to join them in America. I am the middle of five children. I have an older sister and brother, and two younger brothers. When my parents immigrated to the United States, we were all separated. My sister, Trevlyn, and I stayed with my paternal grandmother—my Granny Princess. My younger brother Eldon stayed with my maternal grandmother, Granny Francis. The eldest, my big brother Quincy, stayed with my aunt who lived quite a distance away. Justin was not born yet. We were all basically separated. Being so young, I had no memory of my parents at that time. I had no real understanding of belonging or to whom I belonged. We lived in a small village in Guyana, so although my siblings and I lived in separate houses, most of us were still in proximity to each other, since my grandparents lived across the street from each other.

Between both sets of grandparents, I had a lot of aunts and uncles, altogether thirteen of them. This meant that I also had a lot of cousins, so their houses were never empty. In those days, I was a tomboy; I wanted to do everything my boy cousins were doing. I was a bit of a wild child, and I still have the scars to prove it! Nothing can compare to those days. Despite my desire to be completely wild and free, my Granny Princess always had other plans for me. She has always been a woman of God. She was very serious about church and made sure I was always with her. I have no idea why she always chose me to be the one to accompany her, but I don't remember her making any of her other grandchildren go. At that time, she was the most tangible presence of a mother in my life.

I went everywhere with her, whether I wanted to go or not, and we were in church a few times a week. Do you know how annoying it was to have to go to church when everyone else was still outside playing? I wanted to stay home and play with the other kids, but whenever there was an event at church, my grandmother was there, and I was right beside her. One day, I decided that I didn't want to go to church. My aunt was usually responsible for making sure my hair was done and appropriate for church, and that evening I decided I would hide and not get my hair done. If my hair wasn't done, surely my grandmother would let me stay home. So, I hid and then revealed myself when it was almost time to go to church. When my grandmother saw me, she looked at me and didn't say a word. My hair was completely wild on my head, and I was sure that she would have no choice but to let me stay home. Well, she made me get dressed; my hair was left in that exact state, and we went to church. My grandmother always sat in the front row, so when we walked in, she made me sit in the back of the church, and she walked up to the front and sat down. Needless to say, I never tried that again.

My grandmother taught me church. She taught me prayer and worship. It was a part of me—how could it not be? It was the only way. To this day, I attribute my dedication and devotion to God to the foundation she laid for me. Despite my relationship with my grandmother, there was always a longing for my parents. I had no idea who my parents were, so I had no idea who I was. My first memory was a longing to know them and wondering when they would come for me. My first memory was one of abandonment.

In March of 1986, my father paid a visit to Guyana. I remember it clearly because it was the year I turned five. I have very few memories of his visit because I was so young, but I do remember never leaving his side. In that moment, I finally felt a sense of belonging. It was an exciting time because it was also my fifth birthday, and I remember there being a big party to celebrate it. That experience is highlighted in my memory because I felt as if I had significance—the loneliness I had been feeling was gone. It was hard to say goodbye when it was time for him to leave.

It was two years later that my siblings and I immigrated to the United States and I was once again reunited with my father. The United States was always made to sound like this amazing place with golden streets and all the ice cream you could eat. As a child, that was exciting, and I couldn't wait.

We arrived in Brooklyn, New York, in the middle of a snowstorm on December 11, 1988. When we arrived at the airport, I remember a woman running toward me and reaching out to hug me. I pulled away because I had no idea who she was. Well, it was my mother. I didn't know her; I knew of her but had no idea what she looked like. I remember my younger brother having the same reaction I did. However, I knew my father because he had visited two years before.

Guyana is a tropical country, so going from a warm climate to the frigid cold was something I was not very happy about. What was worse was that no one had prepared me for it. All of the discussions about ice cream and not one about how cold it would be. The United States was quite an adjustment for me. It was cold—the ice cream was good but not worth it! I went from being able to spend my entire days outside to being locked up in an apartment. I hated it, but I was happy to have my siblings and parents in the same home.

I clung to my father, and he spoiled me. My father would always wake up early in the morning and watch television. I would wake up as well and lay right next to him. My favorite show to watch with him was *Popeye the Sailor Man.* That time with my father is one of my fondest memories. My relationship with my mother was not quite the same. We had moments that we shared, and I know I loved my mother, but I just didn't quite understand her. Our relationship always seemed to be combative. I was what they called a very headstrong child. I know I could be difficult at times, and I certainly had a mouth on me.

I don't quite remember how it happened, but one day, my mother turned to me and said, "You're a child people just can't love." I know that it was something said out of frustration and anger, but I don't think she understood how my whole world came crumbling down. Those words would plague me for much of my life and create an internal struggle within me that would be the fight of my life. Those words would lead me down paths of unhealthy, toxic, and destructive relationships. Her words would cause me to build walls and continually push people away in order to not get hurt, because if my mother couldn't find a way to love me, then how could anyone else?

As an adult, I am able to better assess the dynamics of our relationship. My mother was also left to live with her grandmother at a young age when her parents immigrated to London, England. She did not experience much affection but, in fact, endured a lot of abuse at the hands of some relatives. I can imagine she experienced the same feelings of abandonment and a lack of identity that I did as a child. In addition, my parents' marriage was not very healthy. My siblings and I were constantly awakened by arguments and physical fights between our parents at night. I don't remember the cause of it all; I just remember getting to the point where I wanted it all to end. I am not making an excuse for the words my mother spoke to me, but our experience affects the way we function in all of our relationships. If we are unable to confront and work through the traumatic experiences of our past, we are bound to repeat the same patterns of what we have seen.

When my parents announced that they were separating, I remember feeling as if it was for the best. It sounds weird because I was only ten at the time, but that was how awful things had gotten.

When my parents separated, I missed my father more than I even knew how to express. I only remember crying. My mother didn't understand my constant crying, and I had no idea how to express that void. Looking back, and having experienced my own divorce, I don't know how my mom did it with all of us kids. It was difficult for me to do it with just one child. As a kid, I couldn't process my feelings or emotions; all I knew was that I missed my father, and I was confused as to whether or not my mother loved me. My father would pick us up and take us out, just as he would when we all lived together, but it never felt the same. My father and my relationship with him were never the same after that.

A *root is* the beginning of a thing, it's the primary underlying cause of every concept or belief. How we function in our relationships is indicative of the way our relational patterns developed through our formative interactions with others. Recently, I purchased a new home and discovered I have a real love for gardening and landscaping. In fact, I find it to be extremely therapeutic. I also like it because I am able to put my personal touch on my home. I can't do anything else; please don't ask me to try to fix anything. And I am scared of everything creepy crawly. Just tell me who I need to pay to get it done. However, when it comes to being out in my yard, it is my place of solace. I have become obsessed with planting flowers and plants. In the beginning, I started by going to Home Depot and purchasing the already flowering plants, but after a couple of years, I started planting my own seeds and nurturing them until they are ready to grow.

I thought it would be easy to plant the seeds and have them just grow, but I found out it wasn't as easy as I expected it to be. First, every seed is different—some are tiny specs, and others can be relatively large. Like humans, they all require food and water, but each one takes a different period of time to germinate. They start off like us, as little, tiny sprouts that you have to be extremely careful and delicate with. They require a lot of light. The first weeks are extremely important because if you don't care for the seed well enough, it won't take root, and it will be unable to produce a flower. Imagine that we are the seeds. The difficulty is that while my seeds came with instructions, parenting, as they say, does not come with a manual. I know this well because I am a parent.

The manual we receive as parents is typically what has been modeled for us. Some of us parent exactly as our parents did, others do the complete opposite, and some find a healthy medium. Let me bring this home—as seeds, we are not always handled with care, and we are not always given what we need to thrive. These different variations of parenting create our roots. This right here is how our cognitive schema is formed, which is what we reference each time we make a decision about who we are and how we should function. Roots are important because without them you can't thrive; the strength of your roots determines how you will interact and navigate life. I have lived long enough to learn that your ability to thrive in life has nothing to do with how your roots were nurtured, fed, and watered, but by the strength and determination of each individual. As long as you were given roots—good, bad, or indifferent—you have the ability to produce your flower. Your God-given purpose was not determined by what was fed to you, but rather what didn't kill you. You have been so caught up on the roots that you missed the stem and flower that blossomed. You keep losing sight of the seasons that have come and gone, so you miss the strength in each season. If you are alive today, then that root of the past, however bad it was, has strengthened your present. Get mad at it, let the tears roll, but it's true, my dear. Our roots reflect our origin, and if it did not take us out, it made us stronger.

Why is it so hard to find the beauty from our ashes? It's just a thought, not a theological point or even a revelation (it may or may not be), but if God said He would give us beauty for our ashes, and if there are ashes, that indicates the ash is something that you are looking at. You are not a part of what burned up. So that means in order to get the beauty, you, at some point, had to separate yourself from the things that burned; if you hadn't, you would be a part of the ashes. So here, this awesome God of ours is saying, *Let's trade!* I'm going to purchase (on the cross) those ashes from you, and replace them with beauty. It's a hard thing to see the beauty after all the ashes (hurt, pain, rejection, abandonment), but it's possible. I am not speaking to you from a standpoint that self-work is easy work—it's not. Convincing yourself to be able to see the beauty after all the pain is the hardest work you will ever do. However, when that day comes and you are able to see the beauty, it is life-giving and life-changing.

That being said, the root of my relationship patterns began with feelings of rejection, abandonment, and loneliness. These are the roots of my identity. My identity was perceived through stained lenses and an unhealthy foundation. My parental relationships created a lot of hindrances. I spent the first seven years of my life wanting to feel as if I belonged. I believed that once I had my parents, it would lead to a sense of belonging and knowledge of myself. I went from feeling that I did not belong to belonging to a family with very unhealthy dynamics. I had found a place of belonging with my father, but once my parents separated, I no longer had that level of relationship available to me because he left. I struggled to develop a relationship with my mother, never feeling as if she loved me, and wondering how I could possibly be loved if what she said was true: "You're a child people just can't love." This is why I said that I never had a chance. The most formative years of my life were not just a mess; they were utterly devastating.

The depth of your pain is indicative of the depth of your purpose.

In God's interaction with Jeremiah, God spoke first. Likewise, before their words, before their rejection, before they left you, God spoke first.

God has predestined you for greatness! Your experiences and the words that were uttered to you were part of an assignment to deter you from the greatness to which He has called you.

> For we do not wrestle against flesh and blood, but against principalities, against powers, against the rulers of the darkness of this age, against spiritual hosts of wickedness in the heavenly places (Ephesians 6:12).

The depth of your pain is indicative of the depth of your purpose. When God spoke those words over your life, the enemy was there plotting and developing detours to get you off track and cause you to walk in continual negative patterns. The enemy works through people and events to prevent you from reaching God's destination.

Your understanding of yourself is misconceived. Your mother didn't hate you; she was just off track. That relationship didn't kill you; it was a hurdle, not a destination. They didn't leave you; they were just on a different path. Holding on to past hurt and pain keeps you in a perpetual pattern of thoughts and actions that never lead to your intended destination. Instead, it keeps you continually going in circles. This state keeps you from maintaining healthy, functional relationships. Your patterns are inherently rooted in your past.

Chapter 2

Broken Record

*There is no fear in love; but perfect love casts out fear, because
fear involves torment. But he who fears has not been made
perfect in love (1 John 4:18).*

It is very easy for us as women to fall into the trap of saying that there are no good men out there and to blame the man for all the ills of the relationship. Too often, when there is the issue of unrequited love, we automatically assume that the man is cheating, evil, cold-hearted, or just a flat-out dog. It is much easier to deflect the responsibility of a relationship gone bad than to accept any responsibility. Let's be realistic—who wants to admit that they are emotionally unstable?

When you have been on the receiving end of the hurt, it is difficult to recognize that your problem is the type of person you keep choosing to date. Also, you refuse to pay attention to the way you tend to interact in these relationships and, therefore, cannot recognize your ineffective relational patterns. It's so much easier to blame who you believe to be the obvious villain—the other person. If you continually find yourself cycling in the abyss of dysfunctional relationships, something is broken inside of you! What's more significant is that your inability to maintain healthy relationships is directly linked to your relationship with God.

You may be wondering what your relationships with others have to do with your relationship with God. It's through our relationship with God that we gain knowledge of our self or, better yet, our purpose. Your understanding of who you are and what you are created to do will govern every decision you make in life. Your decisions determine your outcome, yielding either positive or negative results. Remember, when the relationship between a person and God is ruptured, our understanding of self is not discernable and there is no longer a clear objective. We independently search to understand who we are through our own exertions and abilities. God's intended pattern is now skewed through our own human efforts, making us deficient and ineffective. We have been trying to operate in these relationships from a place of deficiency.

Is it starting to get clearer to you? It's actually rather simple. Because God created us in His image, when He thought of you, He thought of Himself—He saw you in His holiness, His righteousness, and His power. He saw you as perfection! After the fall of man, our image of self became distorted, and what was once obvious has to be searched out or uncovered. Let's be clear—God's image of you is not skewed, but your ability to see what He sees is blurry. What is blocking your ability to see what He sees?

The answer is simply *life*. Life has happened. Life is filled with many uncertainties. Many women battle fears of abandonment or rejection. Some of us grew up in households that were not nurturing or loving. Our lives have been disrupted by abuse, whether emotional, physical, or sexual. Others grew up in domestically violent households and have watched a parent being brutally beaten by the person who was supposed to love and protect them. There are a number of events and traumatic experiences that can occur in the span of a lifetime. These events alter our perception of healthy functional relationships. They also alter our perception of our self-worth. It is through these experiences that we develop a pattern of behavior or a system by which we do things. Every pattern has a root, every root has a trauma, and every trauma opens the door to fear.

Fear implies that you have not yet been perfected in love. There are certain areas of your life that are broken. Have you ever heard a broken record? What happens with a broken record is that it will play fine until it gets to the part that's scratched or flawed. As soon as it gets to that broken part, it keeps repeating the same verse over and over again. It's the same with your relationships; they will always go well until you get to that place that you haven't quite healed from—that place of brokenness. It can simply be triggered by anything your mate says or does that reminds you of something from the past. This could be a past relationship, a past experience, or even a past trauma. This broken place can cause you to withdraw from the relationship emotionally out of fear of being hurt or an inability to trust. What is significantly apparent is that every time you get to this place, you begin the same patterns; you put up the same walls, and you slowly unravel until you repeat the same outcome.

Every pattern has a root, every root has a trauma, and every trauma opens the door to fear.

Your fears will *always* paralyze you in the plans and purposes God has for your life. The presence of fear is indicative of the fact that you have unresolved issues you have not fully submitted to the healing power of God. By succumbing to your fear, you unknowingly make that fear your idol, thereby esteeming your fear higher than God and creating a gap in your relationship with Him. What's more, the same fears you have about your relationship with your mate are the same fears you hold about God. The only perfect love is God's love. In fact, our love for others can never be perfected outside of receiving the perfect love of God.

Years ago, I began to notice some patterns in my relationships. As I went into a new relationship, each time believing that I was with the man God had chosen for me, my interactions in the relationship began to disintegrate, building on my mistrust and fear of being in a relationship. I couldn't understand how a relationship that would start off so good and seem so ideal would become so destructive. The same person who once told me he loved me would, in turn, be the person who betrayed me. I lost a piece of myself every time, and I lost my confidence. Each time I attempted to put myself out there and not be the bitter woman, the results were always the same. I had three consecutive relationships, and each one ended the same exact way—three completely different men giving me identical explanations as to why they did not want to be in a relationship with me.

In a situation such as the one I just described, it is pretty hard to blame the other person, especially when I was the common denominator in all of my relationships. I had to finally admit to myself that something was broken inside of me. I was a broken record, expecting different results in my new relationship, yet I was still the same person. Constant rejection by others can create insecurities and self-doubt. Inevitably, your insecurities make you vulnerable in relationships and susceptible to mistreatment.

What was the *root* of my relationship problems? Could it have started in my childhood? At the age of five, my innocence was stolen by someone who could not begin to understand how much that one moment would ravish my life. Could this be the origin? Was it from continually waking up to my parents arguing or physically fighting with one another? Or could it possibly be from having someone I loved and trusted, someone who was supposed to protect me in this world, tell me that I'm a child people just can't love? It may be witnessing different abusive relationships throughout your family, where the women are constantly being verbally, emotionally, and physically abused. Whatever the circumstances, we have all experienced some sort of event in our past that traumatized us and left us emotionally paralyzed in certain areas of our lives.

Growing up, I hated the way the women in my family slaved over the men. I couldn't understand why they went to such lengths to try to please them, and in return they were not appreciated. I watched infidelity plague their relationships, yet it was overlooked or ignored. If it wasn't emotional abuse, it was physical. I will never forget one fateful day I visited my aunt's house. I remember how much I enjoyed playing with my cousins and how much fun my aunt was; I admired her. On this particular day, my aunt and uncle had been arguing. I forget exactly what the argument was about, but as he proceeded toward the door, she followed him in an attempt to engage him in conversation. As I sat at the kitchen table, I watched her down the narrow hallway trying to gain his attention before he walked out the front door. He seemed frustrated. In the blink of an eye, he picked up a folded infant stroller and struck my aunt. I saw her fall to the ground and begin to weep. She clutched her back because she was in so much pain. My sister, my cousins, and I all ran to her side. I remember saying, "We should call the police." We begged my aunt to call the police, but she refused. What was most disheartening is that once she was able to get on her feet, her only concern was for my uncle, wondering where he had gone. My aunt acted as if the event had never transpired; however, to me it would be a lasting memory—one that still is not so easily forgotten.

I swore to myself that I would never be a woman who allowed a man to berate and treat me less than I was worth. I would never define myself through the eyes of another individual. The only difficulty with that was that I had no understanding of my true value or my self-worth, so I became exactly what I hated. I found myself in relationships that were emotionally abusive, and I clung to men who used me, cheated on me, and disregarded me. I was a strong, confident woman in every area, except in the area of my relationships. How could I have become what I hated?

I was a mess when it came to relationships. When I accepted Jesus Christ into my life, I then became a glorified mess. Let me explain. I thought that being saved meant I was delivered from my emotional issues. I became very good at glossing over my problems with Scripture, and I attributed my past to just an avenue to minister to others who had experienced similar life events. While it was an awesome avenue to minister from, and God allowed me to speak into the lives of many, I was still broken. My relationships, whether with the opposite sex or not, were complete disasters, and I would soon see that my brokenness was affecting every area of my life.

We are all born into this world with such eagerness to learn. We see this in infants as they love to touch and put everything into their mouths as a way to analyze and understand it. As children grow and are able to verbalize their thoughts, their number one question is *why?* This natural inquisitiveness is how they learn and reason within themselves to determine what is right and what is wrong. They watch our actions and mimic our behaviors. This is how they come to understand the world around them. They depend on their interactions with others to determine what is socially acceptable. It is through these interactions that values and traditions are passed on and their character is formed.

Your character was formed through your interactions and experiences with others. We can never separate ourselves from our experiences. Whether good or bad, they shape our character. You are the sum total of all of your life experiences. Many make the mistake of trying to overlook their past, never really confronting it. Some try to reinvent themselves, becoming carbon copies of someone else. Others simply define themselves through their affiliations and achievements. Then we have those who self-medicate and try to escape their problems through addictions and other destructive actions. The scariest of all are those who lack self-awareness and have convinced themselves they have completely overcome their past. Sadly, many Christians fall into this scary category. We gloss over our emotions and our impairments by quoting scriptures and being overly spiritual.

Second Corinthians 4:16 states, *"For which cause we faint not; but though our outward man perish, yet the inward man is renewed day by day*" (KJV). Paul acknowledges that the outward man, which is our flesh, perishes, but the renewal of our inward man is a daily process. It is not an instantaneous change. The process is different for all of us; therefore, we are not to compare ourselves to others or attempt to be like anyone else. When we are naked and honest before God, that is when He can reveal His heart to us and begin to heal the broken places.

Chapter 3

Image Matters

So God created man in his own image, in the image of God created he him; male and female created he them (Genesis 1:27, KJV).

How you see yourself matters! Image is typically a reproduction or an imitation of a person or thing. It fascinates me every time I think about how God created me to be a reproduction of Him. What is even more baffling is how that could be possible. When I think of God, I think of a perfect Being—perfect in love, perfect in character, and having great assurance of who He is. There was a time in my life when I couldn't picture myself having the ability to be perfect or even fathom the possibility that anyone could ever think of me as perfect.

You will always act out the role of the person you think you are. If you think you are great, you will act as if you are great, and you will inevitably be great. If you think you are weak, you will act weak, and all of your actions will be weak. If you perceive yourself to be courageous, then your actions will be courageous, and you will always be courageous. It sounds simple, but this is actually a hard concept for a lot of us to comprehend. Many of us try to act out the role of the person we want to be, but then we realize that we have played a role we despise.

We are all actors; we work to live up to prescribed scripts we have been given since birth. We don't know ourselves because we have not taken the time to get to know ourselves. Our lives are filled with work, relationships, and activities. We always want to be in the mix, yet the one thing we neglect, or avoid, the most is ourselves. Why do you think we do this? We do this because we are afraid of what we may find. It is a scary thing to look into the depths of your thoughts, your inner fears, and your doubts. Looking so deeply within ourselves disarms us, and we are faced with the reality of acknowledging that we have no idea who the person staring back at us really is.

That image is filled with a lifetime of experiences. It is easy to change our hair, clothing, and career, but the one thing we have yet to figure out is how to change our past. How do you change the past hurts and the trauma of life? It's funny how past events are able to change you, but you have no ability to change them.

For as he thinketh in his heart, so is he (Proverbs 23:7, KJV).

The word translated "thinketh" is the Hebrew word *shâar,* which means to split open a door or a gate. This is referring to a barrier through which people and things pass in order to get to an enclosed area (that hidden place in you). This barrier is not easy to pass through; it is usually a fortified structure, meaning it is extremely difficult for anything to penetrate its walls. The heart is the Hebrew word *nephesh,* which simply means the soul, self, or life. We are the gatekeepers of this fortified structure we call "self." It is instinctual to protect and guard it.

This fortified structure is made up of our defenses; however, it is not impenetrable. We create these defenses when we try to recreate our image. These defenses are created as a way to block out unwanted criticisms or ideologies others might formulate against us. They hide the debris of past indiscretions and give the guise of healed trauma. They blot out insecurities and distinguish irrational characteristics. It is our attempt at creating perfection.

Scripture warns us: *"Keep and guard your heart with all vigilance and above all that you guard, for out of it flow the springs of life"* (Proverbs 4:23, AMPC). Certain translations replace the word *spring* with *issues*. Issues, we all have them! What is crucial is how we navigate our way around them. What will consistently split open the gate to your "self" every time are your issues. The reason most of us cannot perpetrate the lie of our made-up self for too long is because every time we come face to face with our issues, our walls come crumbling down. It is amazing how strong our defenses can be, but all it takes is one word, one memory, or one touch to disarm that fortified structure and render it defenseless. The event that disarms your fortified structure is your trigger. The trigger brings your trauma to the surface. When this happens, everything you have been trying to hide begins to come into the light. Every time you are triggered, you are reminded of the past, and you become so crippled that you open the gates and allow it to take a seat in your life. The repercussions of this can be disastrous.

This is why image matters! Your walls are only penetrable because you believe you are what has transpired in your life. You have validated in your mind every negative word, every abuse, every horrible experience, and you have given them habitation in your heart. Anything you have validated is now an ingrained part of how you see yourself (your image). It is crippling because you believe it! Most relationships usually falter at this point because, in order to build back those defenses, you resort to what is familiar and what is safe: you.

Chapter 4

Understanding Your Trigger

When an impure spirit comes out of a person, it goes through arid places seeking rest and does not find it. Then it says, "I will return to the house I left." When it arrives, it finds the house swept clean and put in order. Then it goes and takes seven other spirits more wicked than itself, and they go in and live there. And the final condition of that person is worse than the first (Luke 11:24-26, NIV).

A trigger is simply something that re-ignites a past experience. Usually, this incident causes upsetting feelings and problematic behaviors that are often associated with a past trauma. The triggering event can cause an individual to revert to old ways or unhealthy behavior patterns. These patterns surface when there is an issue that has not been dealt with in your life.

The reason we revert to these behavior patterns is because they are a part of that *fortified structure*—the walls we have built to protect ourselves and keep unwanted things out. We operate behind these walls in order to keep ourselves safe. The problem is they create barriers in which nothing can go out and nothing can come in. We keep others at a distance, never fully letting them in and never fully giving of ourselves. If we are able to control our level of commitment then, hypothetically, we are able to control our ability to get hurt.

This structure exists in our thinking; it stays alive in the thoughts that replay in our mind. For me, it was the comment, "You're a child people just can't love," and my belief that everyone I love always leaves. In every relationship in my life, I've always expected the other person to leave. It became an innate reaction in me to begin to either pull away or sabotage the relationship I was in. I went into relationships with the constant fear of being hurt. I would anticipate when it would happen and sometimes how it would happen. It is important to understand that we are *not* strategic about our patterns; in fact, we have no idea that we are acting out these behaviors.

At the age of five, as I was taking a nap, my innocence was disrupted. I just remember the shock of it and feeling frozen. I laid there numb, not understanding what was going on or what I should do. This reaction would follow me throughout my adult life when confronted with difficult situations. I remember someone running up the stairs and telling him to stop.

At age nine, while visiting family in Maryland and having an innocent sleepover in the living room, I was inappropriately fondled. I remember just lying there numb. I didn't know how to scream or even say stop. I just laid there feeling violated and dirty. Perhaps the worst and most traumatizing memory happened while we were visiting my aunt's house one summer. My aunt was known for her generosity and always opening her home to family in need. That particular summer, some family members and their son, Dex, were staying there. I can't remember how old Dex was, but he was close to the age of my sister who is three years older than me. He had to have been a teenager, and I was probably about ten years old. Dex would constantly touch me inappropriately, whether it was grabbing my chest or brushing against my private parts in passing. It would happen as all of us would be playing around the house; he would just grab me. He did it in a bullying way, and I remember feeling terrified of it happening. I was terrified, yet he found what he was doing to be funny. On occasions we would visit my aunt, I would hope that he would not be there. If he was there, I remember feeling frozen in terror of him inappropriately touching me. I don't know why that memory is more traumatizing than the others. Maybe it has to do with the fact that it happened on multiple occasions or because of the intimidation factor. However, it planted a seed of fear in me.

Fast forward to my twenties: I was licensed as a minister at a local church in Syracuse, New York. I did a lot of my maturing as a Christian under the microscope of the church. By this, I mean that, as a leader, you do not always have the luxury of messing up and it being concealed. I took the responsibility that God had placed on me as a leader very seriously. I genuinely had a strong desire to do the will of God and live with integrity.

I also loved the people in the church; they were like family to me. When I first joined the church, it was extremely difficult for me to commit to becoming a member. I was always serving and helping out, but becoming a member meant that I would need to commit to staying in one place and being fully invested. To the average person, this is easy, but to an individual who had never known stability—one who has extreme issues with trust—this is significantly difficult. One day, the pastor approached me and said, "Kelsie, when are you going to join the church?" I remember feeling as if the walls in the room were closing in on me. Until he posed that question, I was absolutely comfortable with participating in all the activities and helping out without necessarily being a member. His question made me think; if I were to join any church, it would be that church.

When I entered the doors of that church, I was a complete emotional mess and broken in so many areas of my life. The pastor of the church showed me extreme favor and treated me as a daughter. I looked up to him and loved him as a parental figure. The significance of this was that a major part of my brokenness had to do with a mistrust of parental/authority figures in my life. For the first time,

I found myself trusting and finding safety that I had never felt with any adult figure before.

The next Sunday, when the altar call was made and the invitation to join the church was put forth, I stood up and began to make my way down the aisle. Tears flooded my face, and boogers were coming out of my nose due to the extent of my crying. I remember the altar worker asking me if I wanted to give my life to Christ. I kindly told her that I had already accepted the Lord. The emotional display had everything to do with me making a commitment to be a part of something, deciding to stay in one place for a period of time, and making an emotional investment in which I had to follow through.

A little over a year later, I was licensed as a minister. Three years later, our church was preparing for the annual church conference. I usually tried to help out with the cleaning of the church and making the labels for the CDs. As it was my practice every year, I showed up to the church, ready to help out. I went into the pastor's office to say hello and talk, as was our usual routine, but that day he was different. The pastor seemed cold and aloof. I began to wonder what was wrong and why he seemed so distant toward me. I tried to give the pastor the benefit of the doubt and persist in doing my usual routine to help out. I was told that someone else would be doing the labels for the CDs, and there wasn't anything left to really clean at the church. Another minister, who was the pastor's right-hand man, asked me to accompany him to help pick up some equipment. He and his wife were good friends of mine. I agreed, and we went on our way. As we were driving, he began to tell me how it had recently come to the pastor's attention that there were certain rumors going around in the church. The rumors implied inappropriate relations between me and the pastor. My minister friend continued to tell me that, because of these rumors, it would be appropriate for me to keep my distance from the pastor so others wouldn't get the wrong idea.

Immediately, the same feeling I felt when the pastor first asked me, "Kelsie, when are you going to join the church?" came upon me. The best way to describe it is being surrounded by steel reinforced walls and holding my breath until my heart stopped beating. This was the same feeling I always felt when I realized I had been betrayed by someone I trusted. Although I was physically present in the conversation, the steel walls surrounded me, and a feeling of numbness plagued my heart. That night, I was to be the armor bearer for the main speaker, and I remember my friend telling me to "just act normal." He stated, referring to the main speaker, "You don't want her to catch what you're feeling in the spirit."

In that instant, my world shattered. Until that time, I had convinced myself that I had been delivered from my tendencies, better known as patterns. At this particular conference, I had plans to hang out with one of the gospel recording artists who would be performing. We had met a year earlier and decided we were going to hang out when he came into town. I tried my hardest to gloss over what was going on, but to anyone who was around me, it was apparent there was something very wrong. When we met after the service that evening, he kept trying to get me to talk, but as much as I wanted to talk it out with someone, I didn't think it was in the best interests of the church for me to discuss such a matter with him. We went to the movies, and the date ended early because I just couldn't put the hurt of the situation out of my mind.

On the last night of the conference, I decided to go to the hotel room of the recording artist. I was seeking his attention. I also felt really bad about our date the night before. I wanted to not constantly focus on the hurt I was feeling. I won't tell you that I went to his room looking to be intimate with him, because I didn't. In actuality, I didn't exactly know what I was looking for.

When triggered, I would sink back into my old ways of doing things. I didn't want to be intimate with the recording artist. At the time, he made me feel wanted and showed me affection. As I laid in his bed, I remember feeling numbness as we kissed. I laid there numb, feeling complete conviction mixed with a feeling of complete recklessness. As he kissed me, I felt no emotion, and we almost crossed the line. If he had decided not to stop, I would have continued. Is it because I wanted to be intimate? Was I a whore, or loose? The answer is no! I wasn't looking to be intimate with the recording artist; I was just looking for something that felt like acceptance—something that made me feel wanted. I put up my fortified walls, and for that moment, I didn't want to care anymore. I just wanted to numb the pain.

The day after the conference was over, the pastor called me into his office. Apparently, he was at the hotel the previous night and saw me going to the artist's hotel room. The pastor scolded me about the inappropriateness of my behavior, and he gave me a fatherly talk about loving myself and my self-worth. He closed it off by saying, "I love you." I am absolutely certain he meant it in a fatherly way. I didn't say a word throughout the entire conversation because I knew my actions were wrong. I refused to make any excuse or offer an explanation. Until that point, I had held a persona of having it all together, but now I was exposed. My silence did not mean that I agreed with everything he said; it just meant it was neither the place nor the time for me to speak. As I listened to him, his words were filled with assumptions and characterizations. I still chose not to speak. It was ironic to me, since his actions were what triggered me in the first place.

It was at that point that he changed, and the way he related to me also changed. The relationship (spiritual father to spiritual daughter) changed, and it would inevitably lead to me leaving the church.

The ability to identify your trigger will lead you down the path of discovering the root of your pattern. These incidents, though completely different, reflect the development of a pattern that would influence a large portion of my life. The defenselessness I felt after waking up to someone on top of me, trying to have sex with me, is the same feeling I felt when someone I loved violated my trust. It is a hard thing to make the connection of past hurts with the hurts of the present. What we fail to recognize is that we continually live out the same patterns, only in different scenarios. When trauma hits, my response is usually to just lie there numb.

The point I want to bring home is that our trigger is connected to a feeling or emotion that causes us to remember or go back to a place where we felt disarmed and unsure as to how to protect ourselves (trauma). Notice, the response is always the same. Our responses eventually become instinctual.

Chapter 5

Recognizing Your Fear

Fear is the avoidance of pain. Fear only has power when it is attached to deep pain. If there was no pain attached to your fear, then whatever you fear would have no relevance. In order to avoid pain in a relationship, we never fully give of ourselves. To give of yourself would mean to fully commit and let go and trust another person with the vulnerability of our heart.

My personal fear is rejection. The fear that "everyone I love always leaves" appeared to be my reality. Of course, the person is leaving because I am just not capable of being loved. It appears the thing that attracted people to me, whether good or bad, was my sexuality. With my sexuality, I discovered a way to obtain a feeling of acceptance and being wanted. It was then built into my patterns in relationships, and it was what I used to try to maintain the relationship. It is also the thing I placed worth in, and I worried that if I withheld this thing, the relationship would not be sustained. It is a hard thing to be a Christian woman with a disillusioned system of thinking. You can have the purest heart for God and still not understand your patterns or from where they are derived, which will send you into a perpetual cycle of unhealthy relationships that lead to continuous rejection. The thing you fear is ultimately the thing you will manifest in your life.

The reason you are continuously failing in relationships is because of your unhealthy system of thinking. Your unhealthy system of thinking was developed by the unhealthy relationships and experiences you were exposed to throughout your life. These relationships and experiences played a significant role in shaping your concept of *self.* Depending on the relationships and experiences, your understanding of yourself can become completely marred. If a person has a healthy self-concept, they are more likely to recognize when a relationship has the potential to be unhealthy and then disengage. The person with a healthy self-concept is bolder about setting standards and informing the other person about their likes and dislikes. This type of person has fewer issues with setting healthy boundaries and walking away from a situation if those boundaries are not maintained. An individual with an unhealthy system of thinking is unable to do this; they are too afraid of being rejected, so they allow themselves to be abused.

We fail to realize that we continually live out the same patterns only in different scenarios. Every relationship you've been in, or will be in, will always follow the same pattern. The reason for this is that we have a tendency to take care of what's on the surface and never really deal with the core of the issue. The truth is that the core is too hard to confront. We convince ourselves that the demise of the relationship was for superficial reasons; he was too old or too young, he didn't have enough education or money, or he wasn't on the same level spiritually. So you enter into relationship after relationship with either an extremely long list of standards or none at all. At the end of each relationship, you clean yourself up and vow never to fall for the same kind of person again. Then, you find a new guy who appears to not have the same issue as the previous guy, yet the relationship has the same outcome. Although his issues may be different, yours remain the same.

The constant relationship failures tear down your self-esteem, self-worth, and self-awareness. With each relationship comes a different level of rejection, and you lose a piece of yourself every time. After a while, you are left confused, unsure, and completely scared. Your condition is worse than when you first started dating. In the beginning, you had what you thought to be a clear understanding of who you are, but if you did, the majority of the relationships you've been in never would have happened.

A friend once told me, "Your love is limited." This person had known me for most of my adult life. It was clear to me that, within the context of our friendship, I had let her down. What was even more clear was that I understood exactly what she meant by her statement. From the inception of our friendship, my intention was always to be a good friend to her, but the instant she disappointed me, I closed myself off and only allowed myself to minimally commit to our friendship. This inevitably led to our friendship ending.

I have always looked at the lives of others and wondered why it seems that some people have it so easy. In my life, I have known so much pain, and I have experienced disappointment in almost all of my significant relationships. Love has always been a flawed thing for me. It was in my relationship with Christ that I began to walk in an understanding of what the possibility of love could actually be. He began by showing me His love through His grace, and then He began to tell me that I was loved and capable of being loved. Finally, He began to show me how to trust the love of others.

At one of the hardest times in my life, the Lord spoke to me and asked, "Kelsie, what is your deepest fear?" Immediately, my spirit responded and said, "That You will let me down like everyone else has." I emphasize that it was my spirit that spoke because I consciously did not know, or better yet, I never acknowledged that was my fear. At that point in my life, I felt rejected by my church, my pastor, my family, the person I loved—basically everyone. For months, I was overcome with depression. I would muster enough energy to go to work and then come home and cry myself to sleep.

I told you the story of the gospel recording artist, but what I didn't tell you was that about six months prior to that experience, as I sat in church listening to my pastor preach, I remember feeling very proud of myself. I remember feeling like I had come close to mastering the Christian walk. That moment has always been significant to me because it was then that God began to expose me. God used that event with the gospel recording artist to bring to light my internal struggles. I could no longer hide behind the image I created for myself or how others perceived me. The exposure of my hidden flaws created an environment of rejection that would disrupt the whole foundation of my world.

When God began to expose the flaws in me, I was forced to see beyond the conceit of my deeds so I could fully comprehend the extraordinary power of His grace. It is not an easy task to accept our flaws, especially those we are ashamed of. The reason we are ashamed of them is because they call attention to qualities we have complete and utter hatred toward—the things we have been trying to run from our entire life. We determined in our mind that we would never be that person, and then we did everything we thought possible to not become what we hate. Who wants to admit they have become what they hated?

The event that took place with the gospel recording artist eventually led to the severing of the relationship between my pastor and me. The moment this happened, it planted a seed in the mind of my pastor that, at that time, he just could not move past. The interaction between us changed so drastically and created such an uncomfortable environment that it ultimately caused me to leave the church. My pastor's perception of my actions changed his views of me, and his comments and statements became inappropriate and unhealthy. When I began to distance myself from the relationship, it became emotionally and verbally abusive. He would begin to talk about me with other members in the church, which created alienation among certain members.

One day, one of the mothers of the church contacted me and asked me to stop by her house for us to talk. I had been so overwhelmed by what was going on that I wanted someone to confide in. She had been someone I trusted, and I thought we had a close and trusting relationship. I shared with her everything the pastor was doing—the inappropriate statements and comments, the numerous phone calls, the verbal abuse that would occur if I didn't agree with his statements, the misuse of his authority. I remember feeling relieved that I was finally able to speak to someone about it. I remember her saying to me, "Honey, forgive me, don't be mad at me." I looked at her, unsure of what she was talking about, and I soon realized that the pastor had asked her to speak to me; everything we discussed, she would share with him. The situation was so unhealthy that I began to develop anxiety when going into the church, to the point that I would pray for God's protection before entering the building. I eventually built the courage to leave the church. I was broken and on the verge of losing my mind. The issues I faced with my relationships in the world were now the same unhealthy, hurtful relationships I developed in the church. I felt rejected and abandoned.

I thought the church would have been able to handle my flaws. The problem with that is too often we rely on others to heal our wounds. Fear forms because we begin to use our offense as validation for our perceptions. For me, it was that love is flawed and rejection is inevitable. I couldn't find healthy, loving relationships—not even in the church.

It is not that love is flawed; it is our perception of love that is flawed. God is Love! And God is perfect. What is flawed is our perception of God, meaning we have not built our relationship with Him in order to understand love. So love is flawed in us because we have not spent enough time with Love to understand Love. If we have not spent enough time with Love, then there is no way we can become perfected in it. Love and fear cannot co-exist; one always negates the other. We will either live in fear or we will live in Love. So your issue is with God!

It took eight years after leaving the church, countless relationships that ended, and a marriage that was verbally, emotionally, and physically abusive for me to finally admit to God that I was angry with Him. I was bitter and resentful. I didn't trust Him because I couldn't understand why He would allow all of the pain and abuse to occur in my life when He had the power to stop it. How could He say that He loves me if I had to experience everything I went through? What was so different in my relationship with Him than all the others?

It is okay to be honest about your issues with God. I will tell you a secret—He already knows them. Once He gets you to a place where you are able to recognize them, He can begin to build an in-depth and personal relationship with you. Then you can begin to work toward perfect love.

Chapter 6

The Awakening

At the beginning of my sophomore year of college, my friend Suzie and I were surveying the campus; we were bored and looking for something to get into. As we walked, we noticed a tall, muscular, neatly dressed guy coming toward us. We immediately said hello and introduced ourselves. He cordially said hello back and told us that his name was Rick. It was Rick's first year of college, so we used that to our advantage and got him to purchase tickets for us all to go to the reggae concert that evening. I wasn't interested in Rick at the time; it seemed he was more interested in Suzie. I was okay with that, since I was coping with the loss of what had been a very complicated situation with another guy.

That night, when Rick arrived to pick up Suzie and me to go to the concert, I looked at the way he was dressed and immediately knew that he was not Suzie's type. She felt the same way, so, naturally, we did the old switcheroo. Once we arrived at the concert, Suzie disappeared and left me and Rick to get to know each other. Rick and I did just that; we danced and talked all night. Unfortunately, I had an ulterior motive to my dancing and talking with Rick. The "complicated situation" was also at that concert, and I enjoyed watching him watch me and Rick dance and enjoy each other's company. Rick obviously had no idea this was happening.

Rick and I began seeing each other. Though it was nice to have someone to do things with, I wasn't very interested in Rick. I tried to be, but although he was very open about us publicly seeing each other, in private, I spent the majority of the time fighting his hands off of me. That was very unattractive to me, especially since I was still dealing with getting over the last guy. There were things I liked about Rick, and there were some things that seemed very mysterious.

One day, Rick disappeared. We usually ate lunch together, but that particular day, I couldn't get in contact with him, so I went to lunch by myself. As I selected my lunch and took a seat, I noticed that he was sitting across the dining hall by himself. That was a relief to me because at least he wasn't with someone else. However, the look on his face was so depressing that it was as if he was hopeless and in despair. He looked very depressed and lonely. I remember that, at that moment, a deep fear came over me. I just sat there wondering what he could be dealing with that could have caused so much sadness.

As I watched Rick from across the dining hall, I feared two things: I feared that whatever he was depressed about was bigger than I could fathom, and second, he would always just disappear, and there was nothing I would be able to do about it. I continued to date him, but that moment remained with me.

One day, Rick decided to teach me a lesson. He felt I didn't take him seriously and treated him like he was just a freshman. At that point, we were not sleeping together. The best way I can describe what he did is to say that he got me to the point of vulnerability and then walked away to make his point. That tactic might have worked with another person, but with me, it was all I needed to end things and walk away.

That night, Rick returned to my dorm room, very proud of himself, and sure that I had learned my lesson. I learned a lesson, but it wasn't the lesson he was expecting. I ended things between us. Two weeks later, there was Rick and his new girlfriend in the dining hall, eating breakfast together. The two stayed together throughout our entire college years. Although Rick and I built what seemed to be a very good friendship over those years, I was always a little secretly resentful that he was in a relationship barely two weeks after things ended with us.

He was a great support to me during college, when all of the trauma of life caught up to me. He was always a listening ear, and he made himself available whenever I needed him. This created a dynamic that I wasn't accustomed to. I wasn't accustomed to anyone being there; as a matter of fact, I had felt lonely my entire life. Rick was the first consistent and dependable person I had encountered up to that point.

It is important to understand that I did not have that much to compare it to. As I stated, I grew up hearing the words, "You're a child people just can't love." My relationship with my father had been close, but once my parents divorced, that was never the same. All my life, I felt alone and unloved. With the history of abuse and trauma I experienced, my relationship with Rick was the closest thing to love that I had ever known. He appeared to be more than I had experienced in my past, which made it easy to overlook obvious warning signs in his character. Oddly enough, the more he tried to cling to our friendship, the more I ran away from it. I remember always wondering what he could possibly see in me.

I constantly pushed him away because I always felt that the people I loved would leave. I had built a structure in my head that I was in control of the relationship between Rick and myself. I kept him at a safe distance, never letting him get too close. I controlled when we talked, how long we talked, and the amount of time we spent together. As long as those boundaries were in place, I was good; I was safe from getting hurt. You are probably wondering where his girlfriend was at that time. They were still in a relationship, but I gloried in the fact that I was still able to have that control. I also went back to the complicated relationship. *Complicated* was code for not having a title and being with someone who did not want to commit to me.

Rick would constantly tell me how miserable he was in his relationship and how much he wanted us to be together. He would tell me stories about their issues with intimacy and how confused he was about her love for him. I was also someone with whom Rick felt free to talk about his past. We both knew very intimate details about each other's lives. I perceived him to be this great person, reliable and dependable, but the more it felt like love, the more I feared, and the more I pushed him away. My perception of love was that it always leaves. I believed that once a person really got to know me, they would leave because I was unlovable. I believed I was incapable of being loved. That perception caused the development of an extremely unhealthy dynamic between Rick and me. At the time, I had no idea how unhealthy it actually was.

I continued in my complicated relationship through my college years. It was constantly on-again and off-again. During one of the hardest of the dozens of separations from that person, I called Rick and asked him to come over. It was after midnight, and what they say is true, nothing good ever happens after midnight. I was fed up, and I wanted to be comforted by someone. Although I had never crossed the line physically with Rick while he was in a relationship, that night, I did not care. I figured everyone else was sleeping with the guy I wanted to be with, so why should I care if I slept with someone else's man?

Rick came over that night, and we were intimate with one another, which was something I know Rick had wanted for a long time. I lay next to him, not really knowing what to think of what had just happened. I remember, at that moment, being very vulnerable, and my guard was all the way down. I expected him to say something beautiful that would ease my burdens and allow me to be vulnerable with him. Rick laid next to me and said, "Wow, now I can be in a relationship with Simone and also sleep with you."

I felt numb; my heart slowly began to harden. I kicked him out of my room in the most callous and degrading way I could think of at that time, to pay him back for the words that came out of his mouth. He, on the other hand, had no idea that's what I was doing because that was the way I always treated him. We remained friends, but I never forgot his words that night. Not too long after, I gave my life to Christ.

After graduation, Rick and I kept in contact. I moved to Syracuse, New York to pursue my graduate degree. He still had another year until he would graduate with his undergrad degree. Rick and I would talk sporadically, and from time to time, he would ask me to marry him. He never did it formally or presented a ring, but he would constantly tell me that I would be his wife. Although I would say no, the surety in his voice made me wonder if it was true.

One day, I received a phone call from a friend of mine who called to ask me whether Rick and I had ever dated. I questioned her as to why she was asking me about it, and she told me that she and Rick had been seeing each other. I explained to her the complexity of our relationship and then told her that I recently spoke with Rick and, to my knowledge, he was still in a relationship with Simone. That did not seem to upset her in any way, so I assumed she already knew. I hung up the phone and began to feel a bit of anger and frustration about the call.

All night, the phone call bothered me, and I began to wonder why it disturbed me so much. That was when it hit me; I loved Rick. The imminent thought of him being with that particular girl worried me. I was never worried about Simone because I never felt as if she was competition. However, I could see him falling for this girl. She was pretty, had a great personality, and she was very outgoing. I felt I needed to share this new revelation with Rick, and I did. In hindsight, I understand that I was jealous and didn't want to lose Rick's attention. I built up the courage to tell him that I loved him. I honestly do not remember him telling me that he loved me too. I do, however, remember feeling trapped in that feud. He made sure to tell her what I told him, in such a way as to prove I had an ulterior motive of some sort. I called him and confronted him about the entire situation, and I remember him telling me that he did not have time for it and then hung up on me. A little while later, he called and apologized, but it was too late. I distanced myself from him.

I didn't speak to him for over a year, and then one day, out of the blue, he contacted me and asked if he could come to see me. I agreed. I was living in Syracuse, and it was pretty lonely at times. I was glad to see someone familiar and do something that would break up the monotony of the day. We went out to eat, and that is when he dropped the big news that Simone was pregnant. I remember thinking, *I guess this is not meant to be*. However, he had different plans. He told me that he loved me and wanted us to be together. He assured me that he would take care of his responsibility but wanted to be with me.

As messy as the situation sounds, I was actually entertaining the thought of us being together. At that point, I believed I loved him too. I just didn't know what to do with Rick. I sought counsel from my pastor, and he asked if Rick could leave his pregnant girlfriend to be with me, what did I think he was going to do with me? I understood the pastor's point, but in the back of my mind I felt the pastor did not fully understand our love and all we had shared together. One thing was clear to me though—a baby changes things. I could not put myself in a situation in which the baby would be born and Rick would realize he wanted to be with the child and Simone. I made the decision to let go of Rick and allow him to go through that experience.

Three years passed, and one day I thought about Rick and contacted him. That same week, we reconnected. At that time, he had a two-year-old son. I don't know how it happened, but we went from not seeing each other in three years to being in a relationship in one day. According to Rick, he and Simone had broken up. I thought it was finally our chance to be together.

Our relationship was great for the first few weeks, but then he started disappearing. He wasn't sending the "good morning" texts anymore, and phone calls were not as consistent. I became concerned. I was so concerned that I managed to gain access to his phone records to see who he had been calling and speaking with. The activities on his phone definitely seemed suspicious. There was one number in particular that he was calling frequently. That person was located in Canada. I knew that he mentioned to me that he had family in that area, but the time and duration of the calls just did not seem right. Then one day, I noticed another Canadian phone number on his call records. I finally built up the nerve to call that number, and surprisingly enough, it was the number to a hotel. I called and acted as if I were him and informed the staff that I would like to change the date of my reservation. It was easier than I thought it would be, and I changed the date to an alternate weekend.

I was furious, so I built up the nerve to also contact the other number. A female answered the phone, and I said, "Excuse me, you don't know me, and I don't want to start any trouble, but how do you know Rick?" I went on to say, "This is not something I have ever done, but I don't feel he has been honest with me, and I just want the truth." She then said, "Excuse me! Rick and I are just friends." I didn't believe her; it was something about the way she spoke and handled the entire interaction that wasn't settling. He then found out and called and confronted me about it. He accused me of doing the same thing Simone had done to him not too long before. He claimed the female was his cousin's fiancée and that they were friends. He went on to say how embarrassed he was by what I did, and his family could not believe I did that. I then blamed myself and began to apologize. He was so angry that he hung up the phone. I tried calling him several times, but he never answered. I emailed and texted him but got no reply. I poured my heart out in those emails, practically begging him to take me back.

He disappeared for three months. During the months of waiting, my friendship with Lamar grew. Lamar was a co-worker I found extremely attractive. We had a lot in common, and at the time he was a youth minister and so was I. I was attracted to his attentiveness to ministry. We had a lot of fun together, and being with him was very relaxed and full of laughter. As attracted as I was to Lamar, I never let it go further than us being friends and going out to lunch together. The reason for that was because he was legally married. According to him, he was separated from his wife and had filed for divorce, but she refused to sign the divorce papers. He was the father of two sons, both under five years old. I was intrigued by him, but that was as far as it went.

During that time period, I was going through a lot at my church. The situation was so stressful that it started to affect me physically. I was experiencing gastrointestinal problems, and I had an incessant cough that only occurred when getting worked up or upset. It would often happen when the pastor would call me; it was as if he was losing his control over me, so he would find any reason to call and reprimand me about any and every little thing. He called me at least three times a day, and if I didn't answer, it would turn into an issue about church.

It was then that Lamar became a confidant; I could talk to him about my situations with Rick and the church. Our lunches became a daily thing, and we enjoyed each other's company a lot. Lamar would constantly ask me to dinner, but I turned him down each time. I refused to date a married man, no matter how attracted to him I was.

One day, out of the blue, Rick contacted me and told me he was driving through Syracuse and wanted to see me. I had lunch plans with Lamar but cancelled them to see Rick. It had been three months, and there he was. We were intimate and then he left to stay with his son and Simone. I was so upset that I called Lamar and asked him if he still wanted to go get something to eat. I understood that it was no longer considered lunch; it was evening, and it would be me having dinner with him. I just didn't care anymore. In my mind, I was prepared to be an adulterer too.

I have to interject and set the stage for what led up to these events. Up to that point, I had been celibate for over five years. That was my commitment, not only to God, but also to myself. In those years, of course I had been tempted, but I never broke my celibacy. But I had recently left the church home I had come to love. I left because the situation with the pastor was extremely abusive. He would constantly call me to argue about the craziest things. He was verbally abusive, not only in his tone, but with the words that were coming out of his mouth. He was also borderline inappropriate with me. He would begin to make comments that implied he wanted an intimate relationship with me. That, of course, was traumatizing and completely heartbreaking. I had spent years under the tutelage of that man, but the situation was so stressful I had to step down from my position as a minister at the church. I was so broken that I quit everything. I was pursuing a graduate degree in Divinity, and I had to walk away from that as well. I also gave a letter of resignation to my job without even having another position lined up.

My life had become so stressful that I had to let go of everything that was stressing me out. As I began to let those things go, it was like the burdens were being lifted off of my shoulders, and I was regaining my health. Within a year, my life had completely changed. I walked away from everything I had found security in at that point in my life. I was angry, I was hurt, and I was nearing the point of losing my mind. I had no idea who I was.

Then there was Lamar; he was there at the right time. It was not the right situation, but I needed him at that time. He made me feel beautiful and wanted. With him, I was the person I was before the church tried to mold me into the woman they thought I should be. I was no longer the person everyone called when they needed to vent or dump all of their issues and frustrations. I didn't have to be the responsible one or live up to anyone's standards for me. I was just me, the girl who loved to laugh and joke. He seemed like everything I ever wanted in a man; the only problem was that he wasn't my man. He belonged to someone else, whether they were separated or not. As much fun as we were having, I felt as if I was in the way of any possibility he would have to reconcile with his wife. These were the thoughts that ran through my mind when we weren't around each other. However, when we were together, he made me get out of my mind. For the first time in my life, I was living in the moment, and I loved him for that.

That relationship lasted only three months. One day, Lamar told me he was coming to pick me up and we were going out to dinner. I waited and I called, but there was no answer. I became angry, so I packed up everything I could fit in my car, and I drove to my mother's house during the night. That was originally the plan, but it wasn't scheduled to happen for another few weeks. I was trying to stay in Syracuse for him. I was trying to hold it together for him, though I knew my world was crumbling all around me. He, on the other hand, went on living his life. His life wasn't crumbling; in fact, he was doing just fine. The next morning, he called me and apologized for falling asleep and asked if I wanted to grab breakfast. I told him I was in Middletown. He was upset and said, "You left me?" He repeated that phase a few more times before the end of our conversation. The conversation wasn't the same as it had been in the past; I was spiraling. I had to face life and the fact that I was jobless, churchless, and living at my mother's house. I hadn't lived at home since I left for college. I just couldn't hold on to a relationship, as hard as I tried. Our phone calls dwindled because we just didn't have the same vibe we had before. A week would go by with no communication, and we were down to sporadic texts until, one day, I begged him to talk to me and tell me if things were truly over. Despite the obvious signs, I needed to hear him say it.

He finally called me; we exchanged cordialities, and then he said it: "Kelsie, I'm married." I thought to myself, *Yeah, we covered this already*. He said, "I need to resolve this situation before I enter into a new relationship." He then ended the conversation and told me he would give me a call later. I told him not to bother.

I found a job in Brooklyn and was to start working the following week. I was in Middletown at the time of our conversation. I drove all the way to Brooklyn in complete heartbreak. My mother's house was full of people, which meant that I would not have any privacy to mourn the situation. At my father's house in Brooklyn, I would have all the privacy I needed. I spent the night pleading with God and begging Him to help me. Then God spoke; He said, "My grace is sufficient." I understood at that moment that the season I was in was something I would have to allow God to take me through without distractions.

Rick had been persistently calling me, but that night, I blocked his number. I spent that summer working, coming home and crying, and going to church. I also spent it with my family. I had spent so much time running away from my family because I felt my upbringing had everything to do with the mess of an adult I was. But there was something about being around my family that brought me back to myself. We spend so much time running from what we were, not realizing that the person we were is the only one who can bring us to the person we are to become. We must reconcile our past and our present in order to become all that God has called us to be.

God finally had me alone. I found a great church and drove about an hour each way, every Wednesday and Sunday, but it was worth it.

I stayed and worked in Brooklyn for a few months and then decided to relocate back to Middletown, New York. I hated the job in Brooklyn so much that, one day, I just decided to quit. Brooklyn is a great city to visit, but I can't handle the busyness of it. It was too much of a hassle just to go to the post office, and parking is horrible. I was living at my mother's house again, which was empty because everyone else had gone back to school. My mother worked in Brooklyn and had a second place there. I was still very depressed about everything; Middletown was a perfect hideout. I was unemployed for a couple of months, but I found different activities to keep myself busy.

One day, while I was at home, the doorbell rang, which was unusual because no one ever came to the house, and no one knew I was there. As I walked to the front door, there he was. Rick was driving by and noticed my car parked at my mother's house, so he decided to stop by. Our parents lived half an hour away from each other, so during our college years, we always drove home together on breaks and would hang out together. The perfect set up, I would say. Well, it made for the perfect ideological fairy tale. That evening, we talked, and he told me how much he loved me. He said that I was the love of his life and he wanted us to get married. He was ready for us to fly out to Vegas that weekend. At first, I turned him down and told him that I still had feelings for Lamar. We talked for a while, and then he left.

This did not stop him from dropping by, calling, and texting. He did what he always did; he waited for me to be in a vulnerable place so he could weasel his way back into my life. Rick was living in Middletown, but what he had failed to mention was that his son and the son's mother were also living in Middletown. In fact, they were living together. According to him, they were not in a relationship but were living together for the sake of their son. His son's mother was from Rochester, and at the time it didn't dawn on me that no one would make such a big move for someone they didn't love or someone with whom they did not see a future. In my mind, he was choosing me—I was the one he wanted to marry.

There I was, thinking we had another opportunity to finally be together. That, of course, followed the same unhealthy pattern as always. Rick would disappear because of something he would claim I did or said, and I would blame myself. I always allowed him to make me believe that it was my fault. So, naturally, when he would tell me that my actions made him decide to work things out with the mother of his child, I would profess and plead my love for him and ask for another chance.

This continued for the entire period I was living in Middletown. Throughout my time there, I was frequently looking for jobs in Syracuse. I finally found a job and began to make my transition back there. One day, Rick stopped by and told me he was moving back to Rochester. He failed to mention the part about him moving back with his son and Simone. I was smart enough that I should have figured that out, but instead, I still daydreamed of us being together.

I moved back to Syracuse and decided to leave Rick alone and move on with my life. Before I left Syracuse, I had found a great church, so I returned there. I was focused on bettering myself and healing from everything that had transpired over the past year; yes, it had only been a year! I was doing pretty well for myself. My circle of friends was growing, and I was in a good place.

Naturally, it happened again—Rick texted and said he wanted to come and see me. I agreed to him stopping by, and he came over and gave the same old speech about loving me and wanting to be with me. As always, I fell for it. He told me that he was ready for us to be together, and I agreed that I was ready as well. He told me that he would return on Monday to see me. I made sure to cook and be ready for his visit, and I was both excited and relieved that we were finally going to be together. Rick never showed up. I mustered the courage to call him and ask him what happened. I will never forget what he said to me: "You know I am with Simone." I hung up the phone and severed all communication with him.

Each time I ended things with Rick, my mind would revert back to Lamar. One day, I built up the nerve to text him and ask him if we could possibly meet. He texted back and told me that he no longer lived in Syracuse, but if he was in the area, he would let me know. I stalked his Facebook page, looking for any sign of him returning to Syracuse. It finally happened one day; he was back in Syracuse, however, he never contacted me. That didn't stop me from thinking that Lamar moving back to Syracuse was a sign that we were destined to be together. He was constantly on my mind and in my thoughts. I patiently waited for the Lord to reunite us since Lamar was divorced, and there was nothing to keep us apart.

* * *

I am going to pause to allow you to process these patterns. I jumped from one unhealthy attachment to the next and would go back again and again. Outside of Christ, I was closed off and non-committal, but with Christ I was open and vulnerable, which led to susceptibility. This happens when we do not appropriately deal with and process the issues of our past. We assume that a relationship with Christ means an automatic deliverance from all of our issues, but that is not true! Deliverance does occur when we come into relationship with Christ, but not all things are instantaneous. I want to make it clear that I was not backslidden—I had a great prayer life, I was consistently serving in a ministry at church, I was utilizing and maturing in my gifts, and I loved the Lord.

Relationships, however, were my struggle and obstacle in becoming the woman God intended for me to be. It had nothing to do with sin, but more to do with my mindset.

There were a number of factors contributing to the patterns in my life. The first was that I struggled with the thought of believing that I was a person who could not be loved because I was told so at a young age. My fight to prove that was not true perpetually kept me in abusive relationships. I would hold on to the verbal profession of those men, never paying attention to their corresponding actions. If I were to let go of the hope that I was loved by someone, then it was true—I could not be loved.

Second, I grew up believing that everyone I love always leaves. Again, letting go meant accepting that this was true, and since I was a person people just couldn't love, it was my fault that they were leaving. I believed I was always the cause and continually begged and apologized for what I perceived to be my mistakes. I couldn't let go of a relationship because I blamed myself for its demise, so I found myself explaining my past and how much it affected me. I was constantly apologizing for who I was because I viewed myself as marred, damaged, and something to apologize for. I was an easy target.

Third, the patterns I exhibited were all I had ever seen. As much as I hated seeing those unhealthy patterns while growing up and swore I would never be that woman, I became exactly what I hated. Hate does not eliminate a behavior; confrontation does. Hate conceals, but confrontation reveals and then heals.

And last, I prayed. I was praying throughout all of these events. I thought for sure that when the guy showed up or called immediately after a prayer, it was a sign from God. I want to debunk the concept that a person must be living in sin to function unhealthily in certain areas of their lives. We are imperfect beings, walking toward perfection while living in an imperfect world. Wisdom without understanding is futile. I can know that I should not be doing something but still lack understanding as to why I do it in the first place and why it is relevant for me to stop this behavior. It was my pattern to cling to anything that looked or felt like love, with a very superficial and minimal understanding of what love truly is and what its actions look like. I have read 1 Corinthians 13 over and over again, but I was void of understanding its references. Your ability to hear God's voice is hindered in the area of your struggle.

* * *

Years after I severed all communication with Rick, I received a false diagnosis that I had an STD. This STD was not one that could be easily treated and go away; it was one that I would have for the rest of my life. I was devastated and wanted to die. Many thoughts ran through my mind, and I was angry. Additionally, I had a brief moment in my brokenness where I decided I was going to just focus on me, and this was my outcome. I wondered if all the other years I spent celibate weren't enough for me to get a pass for my minor indiscretions. Based on the time frame, I decided I needed to contact both Rick and Lamar; it was the responsible thing to do. I also needed to know who had given it to me. It was easy to pinpoint a time frame, and since I wasn't sleeping around, it could have only been one of two individuals.

It had been a year since I spoke with Rick. I wrote him a very accusatory email because I was certain he was the one who had given me the STD. I wasn't very nice at all. For Lamar, on the other hand, I wrote a gentler email, explaining the tragic circumstances. I was sure it was Rick and not Lamar. I received a reply from both men. Lamar's response was very callous, *It wasn't me*. Rick, on the other hand, expressed more happiness to hear from me. He also responded that he did not have an STD.

Rick began his spiel again about missing me and how much he cared for me. He told me about all he had experienced since we last talked. It turned out that he was no longer with the mother of his child; in fact, he had moved back to Middletown. He lost his job and was not in a good place. We talked for hours; it was comforting to me to hear that he would still consider being with me even after knowing that I had contracted an STD. I was later cleared of this diagnosis by another doctor. The original doctor's office accidentally gave out false STD diagnoses. I found this out because a very good friend of mine went to the same doctor's office and also received the same disturbing diagnosis. We were both cleared and never actually had that issue.

Rick and I were inevitably back together, and once again my life, which was starting to make sense, was disrupted. I was confused about how Rick fit into my life. Up to this point, Rick had not been much of a churchgoer, although he promised he would go to church with me. Again, I was faced with the temptation of fornicating after I had been celibate for so long. He also began to tell me about his hardships, and before I knew it I financed a car for him, purchased clothes for him, and loaned him money. I didn't hesitate to do this because I had completely blocked out all that he had put me through. I only thought about the friend who would stay up all night and talk to me while we were in college.

One night, I said to Rick, "Let's get married." He said yes, and within two weeks, we were married. A co-worker of mine was the wife of a pastor, so we had an extremely small ceremony in their church. There was no family, only a couple of my friends who were our witnesses, the pastor and his wife, another co-worker and her husband, and my roommate at the time.

A friend of mine booked a one-night stay for us at a really nice hotel as a wedding gift. It was our first night as a married couple, and I was very excited. I was ready to do what newlyweds do on their wedding night, but Rick was a little frazzled. He then yelled at me for putting too much pressure on him. I remember going to the bathroom, crying, and asking myself, "What have I done?"

Rick's outburst would be the first of many. The first major one happened two weeks after our wedding day when we were looking for a new apartment to rent. We went to view the first apartment and, once I saw where the apartment was located, I told him I would not be comfortable living there. I thought we were having a discussion, but he went off on me. He began to tell me how difficult I was and brought up things I had confided when we were just friends. He then said that I am the reason people leave and don't want to be around me. He started naming friendships and relationships that I had lost and stated that I was to blame for them. I remember sitting quietly in tears. For a while, that was typically how arguments went. I spent a long time not arguing back because I was not the arguing type, and I could not imagine speaking to him the way he spoke to me. Eventually, I got tired of it, and I would try to hurt him as much as he was hurting me. That didn't last very long because I didn't want to be that person who would cause harm to the person I'm supposed to love. So when I couldn't speak outwardly, I began to retreat inwardly. I stopped talking and sharing my feelings with him. Ironically, the thing that I came to love him for, the safe space he created for me to talk and share my thoughts and feelings, was the first thing that went away after we were married.

Rick was verbally, emotionally, and mentally abusive. The marriage lasted a total of six and a half years and ended with him physically assaulting me. Over the course of our marriage, I had been called every derogatory name that could be thought of. Rick continually used the things that I confided to him to manipulate and gaslight me. I was constantly being accused of cheating, so we had many arguments about fictitious males. If he was not arguing, he was isolating himself due to what he called "cloudy" days. Cloudy days were typically depressive episodes, much like what I witnessed in college with him at the dining hall, only now I was living with it. When the cloudy days occurred, he would avoid being in the same room as me and mainly sit on the couch sulking for days. There was no peace because we would argue at least every two to three days. The arguments always centered around his needs not being met, and it seemed the only times we would not argue were the times I chose to keep silent.

I always wondered why he married me; did he have actual feelings for me, or was I just a way out of a bad situation? I remember one day sitting in our bedroom and watching TV while Rick was down-stairs watching TV on the couch. I decided I would go downstairs and lay on the couch with him and watch TV to spend some quality time together. I sat with him for about five minutes before he got up and went upstairs. When I realized he wasn't coming back downstairs, I went up and saw him sitting on the bed watching TV, so I went on my side and sat to watch it with him. Within fifteen minutes or so, he went back downstairs. I then knew that he was trying to avoid me. That behavior was typical for him, except when he wanted to have sex. He would muster up affections for about five minutes, and then he was ready to have sex.

Sex with Rick was like starring in a pornographic film that you didn't know you were a part of. In the beginning, he wouldn't even take my clothes off, just enough to do his business, and then he was done. There was absolutely no intimacy. One day, I attempted to talk to him about it and mentioned the fact that he didn't kiss me or even look at me when we were having sex. He hadn't noticed. He said something very interesting; he told me that he wasn't thinking about me when we had sex. I would soon come to learn about his addiction to pornography, which explained a lot. Through further discussions and instructions, he would learn how to be more present during the act of sex, which made it more pleasurable for us both. I use the word *sex* because that's what it was. There were two occasions in our marriage when we made love. It was those rare moments when he allowed him-self to be vulnerable with me. We had brief moments of vulnerability when he felt like the friend I once had. They were always short-lived, but it gave me a taste of what our marriage could be.

The abuse went from verbal outbursts to small physical acts. One day, as we were arguing, Rick took his fist and punched a hole in the wall. He then proceeded to get in my face, hovering over me and pointing his finger in my face as he yelled. It was then that I decided I needed to get out of the marriage. We had not been married a year. I left and went to my mother's house, determined not to go back to him. That week, I found out I was pregnant. My thoughts of leaving him immediately changed. I thought that given there was a baby on the way, I needed to give our marriage a second chance. So I went back. I lost the baby at nine weeks but did not find out until I was at my twelve-week appointment. I had been extremely sick the first weeks, and all of a sudden it stopped. I was slightly worried but convinced myself that it was because I was entering the second trimester. On the day of my first ultrasound, I remember being excited to see the baby, yet in the back of my mind, I had a nagging feeling. The minute the sonographer started and I saw that little shriveled up circle on the screen, I knew that my fear was true. The sonographer ran out of the room to get my doctor, leaving the lifeless picture on the screen.

The moment you realize you are pregnant, an instant bond is formed between you and the precious life that is cohabitating in your body. It is an instantaneous love, and I had "her" for nine weeks. The week after I found out the pregnancy had ended, I had to have a procedure to remove the fetus since it did not happen naturally. The week leading up to the procedure, I was so hurt. That hurt was unlike any I had ever felt before. I became really sick with the flu, and I was lying in bed sick and hurt. The first day, Rick comforted me. However, the next day, he began to complain about how dirty the house was. That started an argument, and I began to complain about him constantly stressing me out and it being why I miscarried. The day of the procedure, I was placed under anesthesia, and all I remembered was coming in and out of the anesthesia saying, "I want my baby. I want my baby." That was the first time I uttered those words out loud. I don't remember much, but I remember bits and pieces of Rick and the nurse looking at me as if I was putting on a show and they couldn't understand my behavior. I could care less about the nurse, but his callous behavior I couldn't understand.

It finally happened; up until that point, I thought I had endured a lot, but the miscarriage broke me. The pain was insurmountable, and it felt as if I was experiencing it alone. For almost a year, I would have moments when I would just break down and cry. I never knew when it would come, but when it happened, it was crippling. Something in me died, and to this day, as I write this book, I don't quite believe I have gotten that part of me back. I felt abandoned, and at the time I needed Rick the most, he was the most cruel. That is when bitterness began to develop in my heart. I became secretly bitter toward Rick and bitter toward God. I recognized my bitterness toward Rick almost immediately, but it took me a while to acknowledge the bitterness that had formed toward God.

Not too long afterward, Rick and I moved to Connecticut. His father and sisters lived in Connecticut. Our time there was filled with some of the hardest moments for me. I didn't have any family or friends in the area, so my socialization was limited to his family and the couple of friends I made at my new job. The abuse became worse and increasingly more threatening. I had never experienced such pain in my life and became extremely depressed. I contemplated death on a regular basis, begging God to take my life. I remember leaving work one day, and I had the thought of wanting to jump in front of a moving truck. I had become the epitome of the type of woman I hated and promised myself I would never be. The hardest part about processing my marriage, and the events that took place, was acknowledging that I was a woman who fell susceptible to a domestically violent relationship. It was hard to acknowledge this because I spent so many years working with women in similar situations and talking them through the cycle of abuse in order to help them acknowledge they were in an abusive relationship. How did I become this woman? This was my question to God.

I became pregnant for the second time, and my daughter, Olivia, was born a little over a year after the miscarriage. The marriage was still extremely abusive; it didn't stop when I was pregnant. I was constantly being threatened; I had things thrown at me, and I would try my hardest to not feed into the arguments out of fear of another miscarriage. I had blamed Rick and the stress of the marriage for my first miscarriage, and I wasn't willing to allow those stressors to make me miscarry again.

When Olivia was born, I once again saw purpose for my life. I poured everything I had left into loving and caring for her. To this day, I always say, "My daughter saved my life." I longed for love—to be loved and to experience it. As odd as it may sound, one day, as my daughter sat in her car seat and I sat next to her, I noticed how intensely she was staring at me. It was at that moment that I finally had a revelation about love; I realized that love is not something to be earned or something you have to work for, but rather, love is something that can happen naturally and instinctively. All my life, I felt unloved, and that I was someone people just couldn't love. In that moment in the car, my beautiful baby girl dispelled that.

* * *

The marriage continued to be tumultuous to say the least, and I suffered from postpartum depression. I have heard stories of women wanting to cause harm to their child, having harmful thoughts, or not being able to bond with their child. This was not the case for me; I was just depressed. I made sure to never expose it to my daughter; I was too afraid of countertransference. I didn't want my baby to sense my depression. Rick was traveling back and forth to work from Connecticut to Middletown. I would be with the baby all day, from morning until night. He would come home and didn't even want to give me any relief so I could take a bath. For her entire infancy, he changed less than a handful of her diapers—literally less than five diapers for the entire twelve months.

My mother would stop by often to visit and help me with the baby. She was only about an hour and a half away, so she would make the trips. I loved those days; it would give me the opportunity to have moments to myself. Those moments would be trips to Target, but they were still moments I desperately needed. I remember one day, as my mom was about to leave, something in me knew that if she left, I was not going to be able to physically handle caring for my daughter. I was having spells where I would black out and wake up sweating profusely. As she was about to leave, I was more vulnerable with her than I had ever been in my life. I told her that I didn't think I could make it on my own that night. She called out of work and stayed with me. That's when I finally began to tell her all that was going on. Her advice to me was to not argue back, and sometimes I needed to just stay silent. I knew this was the way many women handled those types of marriages. It was the same advice I was given by Rick's mother when I confided in her.

Needless to say, that advice doesn't work. Eventually, it all came to a head one night. Rick came home from work. I had prepared dinner for him and was determined to have us reconnect. He came home and ate; we talked and had a lovely time. It wasn't too long after that he got up and told me he was going to his sister's house. Something in me did not believe it. After he left, I dressed my daughter, who was four months old, and got into the car. I drove across town, looking for his car. But his car wasn't parked at his sister's house. That was the moment I lost it. I went back home, put my daughter to sleep, and took his work shirts out of the closet. I took a permanent marker and spelled the word "LIAR," writing one letter on each shirt. I hung them up right in front of the entry door. I took all of his other clothes and lined the basement floor with them (he usually came in the entry door in the basement).

I grabbed a small knife and placed it in the crease of the living room couch because I was sure he'd probably come after me once he saw that. The reason I chose his work shirts was because he prided himself on his work and appearance. When he entered the door, he became angry and came after me with a knife as I sat on the couch in the living room. He placed it to my neck. I didn't believe he would actually use the knife on me, but then again, maybe I should have been more scared. He eventually went back into the basement, and I locked him out of the house. The next thing I knew, there was a knock at the door. It was the police. He called the police. Rick told the police that I was being domestically violent toward him. The police saw my size, compared it to his, and began to have doubts about his story.

The state of Connecticut is a dual arrest state. This means that in cases of domestic violence, they arrest all parties involved, whether victim or perpetrator. The police were about to arrest me, but because I had a four-month-old baby, they gave me a conditional arrest in the form of a ticket to appear in court the next morning. We were separated for a short period of time with restraining orders in place. To sum it up, the charges were eventually dropped because neither of us had a prior record. We began therapy and tried to work on our marriage. At that point, I was done with Connecticut and was adamant about moving back to Syracuse, which we did once the court proceedings ended. A year later, we were separated. We never know when our moment of awakening will happen. It is a hard thing to pinpoint.

Chapter 7

Clarity in Chaos

Your fear hinders your ability to trust God. We have been conditioned to never admit or acknowledge our mistrust in God. I spent years in bondage, unwilling to admit how much I resented God for everything I had experienced in my life.

Jeremiah 18:1-4 states:

> The word which came to Jeremiah from the LORD, saying: "Arise and go down to the potter's house, and there I will cause you to hear My words." Then I went down to the potter's house, and there he was, making something at the wheel. And the vessel that he made of clay was marred in the hand of the potter; so he made it again into another vessel, as it seemed good to the potter to make.

When God called Jeremiah, He said, "I formed you." "Formed" is the Hebrew word *yatsar.* In Chapter 18, the word "potter" is also the Hebrew word *yatsar,* meaning *formed* and *potter* are derived from the same root word. The word "house" is the Hebrew word *bayith,* which is used 2,055 times in the Bible, meaning house, household, home, temple, prison, place, family, within, and dungeon, interchangeably.

God sent Jeremiah to the potter's house, which can also be called "the place of formation." The place of formation means that sometimes the very house I live in can be my dungeon, my temple, or even the place I worship can be my prison. Even my family, my own flesh and blood, can entrap me. Not to mention, internal conflicts can imprison me. In essence, while in the place of formation, the things and the people closest to me, and even those deep things within me, will bring me to the place where I can finally hear God. Everything you have experienced up to this point has been molding you! The place of formation is simply life, and God allows Jeremiah to go to—or better yet go through—it to get clarity.

The prophet Jeremiah is told to go to the potter's house, *"There I will cause you to hear My words."* How is it that in all the previous chapters, we see Jeremiah proclaiming and declaring the Word of God, and yet, in this scripture, God tells Jeremiah to go to the potter's house where He will cause him to hear His Word? The process of formation takes you to a place where you can no longer uphold those fortified walls you've built. It brings you to a place of utter surrender, rendering you completely undone. It is a place of weakness where your own exertions are not sustainable, and all you have left is total dependence on God. In the midst of all of your life experiences, you were also experiencing God. It's not a matter of *God, are You real?* but rather, *Why have You done this to me?* It's personal! It seeps into your own personal relationship with God. There comes a point in every relationship that, when challenged, in order to go to another level, the depth must be tested.

Surface level relationships are safe; they require no effort. Relationships that have depth take work. These relationships are transparent, naked, and raw. God already knows you; it is you who is deficient in understanding yourself. You can serve God and function in the things of God, but still have relational issues with Him. In the midst of serving God and doing His work, the constant attacks, circumstances, the wait, and not seeing the manifestation of His promises can cause bitterness and resentment to develop. It is possible that so many seasons of pouring into others with no one pouring into you can leave you feeling empty. It is possible to provide clarity to the past hurts of others but still harbor resentment toward your own.

In the presence of bitterness, resentment, anger, and frustration, you want to convince yourself that your issues are with people, but in actuality they are with God. It is God who made you the promise that He will never leave you nor forsake you. Where was He when the abuse happened or when the rejection and abandonment occurred?

The absence of understanding creates internal conflict. Internal conflict produces a double mind, and a double mind is unstable in all its ways (James 1:7-8). So you become disingenuous in the things of God. You begin to speak words you don't actually believe. Because of this, the character of God often suffers from a case of mistaken identity. How can you find comfort in the Comforter if you perceive Him to be the cause of your afflictions?

The place of clarity is also the place of derision, meaning clarity will come out of the place of derision (scorn, mockery, contempt, disdain, ridicule). The hardest situations of our lives are also places where clarity can be found. It is in this place that we are able to see what we are made of and what others are made of. It is at our lowest place that we release control and truly see who is in control.

God is not always the orchestrater of circumstances, but He is often the facilitator. In group dynamics, a facilitator's role is to help make it easier for the group to arrive at its own answer, decision, or conclusion (meaning get to the intended goal). The facilitator knows what needs to be accomplished and encourages full participation, promoting mutual understanding and cultivating shared responsibility.

It is important that your characterization of God be correct. You will not be able to trust God if you perceive Him to be your abuser. A relationship cannot thrive when there is a misconception of roles. If you misunderstand your role in a job, you will not function well in that position. You were hired for a specific purpose to complete a specific task.

If you do not complete that task, you will more than likely be fired from your position.

Your position in God is irreplaceable! In order to function in the role you were designed for, you must understand your purpose; you cannot understand your purpose outside of God. Once you begin to accurately perceive the character of God, you can then begin to trust Him to unfold to you your true self.

I will say it again; God is not your abuser! He has been working in the midst of your unhealthy patterns, intervening, and working on your behalf to get you to arrive at an understanding of who you are. He is waiting for you to come to the conclusion of what He already said. He is waiting for you to decide whether you will believe His report or what others have said or done to you.

> We were burdened beyond measure, above strength, so that we despaired even of life. Yes, we had the sentence of death in ourselves, that we should not trust in ourselves but in God who raises the dead, who delivered us from so great a death, and does deliver us; in whom we trust that He will still deliver us (2 Corinthians 1:8-10).

Paul is saying that in the midst of great hardship, he wanted to die; but the same God who delivered us in the past is delivering us now and will deliver us in future. Like Paul, what I went through happened that I should not trust in myself but in God.

Rick and I were separated. I finally decided that I couldn't stay in the marriage any longer. When I made this decision, we were living in one of the nicest neighborhoods in the area. We were renting a house at a ridiculously high monthly cost, but in Rick's eyes, we had arrived. I was not so sure about that, but the house was everything I had ever wanted in a home. We were renting, so it just didn't feel like it was ours. It was bittersweet because, despite loving it, it was a cause of contention. Rick was so obsessed with looking the part of a happy family that he was willing to have us rent a house that, despite our sizable income, placed us at a disadvantage monthly. We were what they termed "house poor." I was bitter. I had just taken a job that paid extremely well but was stressful, and I faced a lot of adversity within the culture of the job. I wanted to quit but couldn't, because we needed to afford that house. I was stressed out at work; my daughter had just turned a year old, and Rick might have been in the house but was not at all a participatory parent. Despite doing the majority of the work caring for our child, working a stressful job, and doing all of the cooking and cleaning, the expectation was that I should always be ready for intimacy when he was. He was extremely verbally and emotionally abusive toward me, and I had just about had enough of the abuse.

I tried everything to please him and be a good wife; I did it all—the cooking, cleaning, and caring for our child, on top of working a full-time job—but nothing was ever good enough. He was a tormented soul, and it seemed I was the only person he could take it out on. One night, as he stood over me, screaming insults and berating me, I remember looking at him and thinking to myself that there was nothing I could ever do that would be good enough. At that point, I was absolutely positive that I had done all I could do to be the wife he wanted, despite the continuous denial of my needs. Heck, I didn't even recognize the woman I was looking at in the mirror. The vibrant, charismatic personality was feigned, and all that looked back at me was a sad, depressed individual who was riddled with anxiety. Who had I become, and how could I have let myself become that woman? The only solace I experienced was when Rick went to work. He worked out of town, so every week I would get a couple of nights to breathe. My daughter kept me going; I poured everything I had left into her to make sure she never saw me as depressed or sad.

When Rick would return from work, I never knew who would be coming up the stairs. Sometimes he would be in a good mood, and other times, as he entered the house, I could feel the warfare. I knew that an argument or a complaint was coming. One night, he came home and wanted to talk about how we could improve our marriage. I was over these conversations because he never actually listened to my concerns and needs; the discussions usually centered around his needs and how I needed to do better. Those discussions became so unbearable that I stopped talking. I couldn't entertain them anymore. One night, as he talked, I got up and went to use the bathroom as he was speaking. That made him extremely angry because he felt disrespected. It caused him to blow up and, as he was arguing with me about getting up and using the bathroom as he was talking to me, I began to laugh because it was hilarious to me. That, of course, made him even more enraged. He asked me to leave our bedroom, and I looked at him as if he was crazy. He then persisted to drag me from our bed and across the hall of the top floor of that beautiful house that we were paying way too much money to rent on a monthly basis. He dragged me into another of our four bedrooms. As he dragged me across the hall, I remember looking up at him, and it was as if he was outside of his body. I swear I saw his eyes roll back behind his head. He then tossed me into the room, went back to our bedroom, and locked the door.

He awoke the next morning with no remorse. He got dressed and went back on the road. There was no communication between us. He disappeared again. He was angry at me and refused to answer his phone; he was gone for more than a week. Later, he would tell me that he needed a break. It was then that I decided I could no longer live in a marriage like that. I made up my mind that it was over. He moved out, and I found a more affordable place.

For a while, it was nice to have peace. I didn't have arguments or the constant demands and unrealistic expectations that had been placed on me. Of course, it was not easy being a single parent. All of the work and responsibility of raising a child fell on me. It was a big adjustment.

It wasn't too long before my mind started wondering about Lamar and what he was up to. Over the years, I would stalk him on social media. I would constantly think of him, and I always wondered what my life would have been like had I married him. Of course, I blamed myself for the demise of the relationship, despite the fact that he was still married while we were dating. My pattern of always thinking it was my fault that people leave kept me blaming myself in every conflictual situation. I felt a strong desire to have closure and explained to him how emotionally incapable I was of handling a relationship at the time we were dating. The breakup with him was one of my biggest regrets. I was thankful for social media because I was able to get in contact with him. I had overlooked the fact that he was engaged. I assumed that I still had time. I thought that once he talked with me, the memories of how great we were together would come flooding in, and he would realize that he never stopped loving me. Sadly, these were my actual thoughts. Lamar was pastoring a church, which was perfect because it tied into the call on my life. I was purposed to be a leader in the church. I knew that I was always supposed to be a pastor's wife; at least, that's what I made myself believe.

I blamed my marriage for steering me off the course of the calling on my life. I made the wrong decision; I should have chosen Lamar. I eventually left my church and began going to Lamar's church. We eventually connected, and before I knew it, I was having relations with Lamar. I was still married, and he was engaged. I wasn't proud of it; in fact, I had no idea how I had gotten myself in such a mess. I just remember wanting to be wanted. I wanted to feel the emotions I felt years before with him. Years ago, when we dated, the relationship felt like love—the kind I always knew was real but had never experienced until I met him. Again, I was unknowingly searching for proof that I could be loved. I detached myself from one unhealthy situation and attached myself to another.

It pains me to be this vulnerable and transparent in this book, but to gloss over the cyclical patterns would be an injustice. The goal is deliverance. The Word says, "They triumphed over him by the blood of the Lamb and by the word of their testimony" (Revelation 12:11, NIV). Many will read this and say, "She knew what she was doing." Some may even think I was fully knowledgeable and responsible for my actions. They would be right, but what must be understood is that when a person is functioning in a destructive pattern, it paralyzes logical thought. The person's past trauma is triggered, and they begin to work to find that safe place again. The inability to find that safe place will factualize their fear: *I am someone people just can't love.*

A pattern is a repetitious, consistent sequence of behavior that manifests itself the same way every time. Unhealthy patterns exist apart from clarity. Unhealthy patterns are void of revelatory knowledge. Derision creates a state at which an individual no longer has control of their circumstances, therefore rendering their circumstances to be out of their control. Patterns are obsessive mechanisms that we create in order to control our lives in such a way that it creates the illusion of a safe place or a fortified wall that protects us from the irrational reality our mind has produced. What does that mean? It means that we are simply working to protect ourselves through our patterns, but in actuality, it is a deception that hinders and is even more harmful to us. Derision breaks up patterns because, despite a desire to function in a pattern, it places us in unchartered waters.

Derision stirs things up. For example, if you are making a cold beverage and you add sugar, to dissolve the sugar faster, you would need to stir it. Stirring the beverage causes the sugar to dissolve faster because of the kinetic energy that increases the temperature. Smaller granules of sugar will dissolve faster. Stirring keeps the sugar particles in motion, increasing the chances of collision (impact, crash, conflict) and increasing the rate of reaction—the response or result. In order for God to dissolve unhealthy patterns in your life, the only way for Him to do that is to get you out of your norm and stir some things up. He has to put some heat to the problematic area. The stirring keeps things in motion, causing you to eventually get to the place where you hit what they call "rock bottom," and you crash. The impact increases the rate of your response. It causes you to wake up. It is time for you to wake up!

The situation with Lamar was extremely hurtful. He was my pastor; I was serving in his church, and we had also made the mistake of sleeping together. He alluded to being confused about who he loved—his fiancée or me.

One night, I awoke from my sleep and sat in my apartment with my daughter sleeping in the bedroom next to mine. I began to think about everything that had transpired in my life—my marriage and pending divorce, the hurtful situation with Lamar, the sexual abuse, the miscarriage, being told I was a child people just can't love, the constant hardships and rejections, and I finally mustered up the courage to ask God, *"Why?* Why did You allow all of those things to happen to me?" My whole life had been one traumatic experience after the next. This book only focuses on one area of my life; there is a lot that I have left out. It was in that moment that I realized how angry I had been—not with Rick, not with Lamar, not with my parents, but with God. If He loved me, why did He allow those things to happen to me? I had so much bitterness stored up in my heart against God, and it was not until I was broken enough to ask Him that the process of healing began. I would love to tell you it caused an immediate deliverance, but it didn't. My moment of clarity came about a year and a half later.

Lamar ended up getting married the same week he finally admitted he still loved me. The hurt was unbearable and catapulted me right back into the arms of Rick. He said all the right things and offered the comfort that I needed at the time. I have to admit, I wanted to do something to gut punch Lamar; and at the same time, I was faced with the possibility of being alone again. The day I was to sign my divorce papers, I allowed Rick to convince me that we should give our marriage another try. This was the same man who dragged me across a hallway, cursed and called me all types of derogatory names, and threatened to hit me many times during our separation. I took him back. The reunion was really nice for the first few weeks, but then the cycle began all over again.

A year and a half later, Rick and I decided to do an actual honeymoon to Las Vegas after all our years together. I was excited. I'd never been to many places, so it was exciting to get away. My sister and my niece came and spent the week with my daughter while we were on vacation. I must admit, we had a nice time, and I almost felt myself letting my guard down and allowing myself to let him in. In true form, it was short-lived. The night before we were to fly home, Rick got drunk and came to the room when I was asleep. He began to talk about his past and why he can't trust me. I lay in bed angry; I had reached my limit. I was tired of being the trash can for the downloading of all his trauma and then being blamed for his inability to want to work through it in a healthy way. I awoke still feeling angry, so naturally, when he wanted to have sex, I said no. It set him off, and he used all types of superlatives and insults. I looked at him and, for the first time, I realized he would never change. I remember in that moment being silent and not rebutting his comments. There was something in my silence that was almost supernaturally imposed. His behavior that morning was on another level of anger and cruelty.

We flew home, hardly speaking to one another. When we arrived, it was midnight, but my daughter was still awake. I put her to bed and ate some leftovers. Rick said he was hungry and needed something to eat. That was the first full sentence he had spoken since Vegas. I ignored him. I put my daughter to sleep in our bed and then laid down. Rick came into the room and also laid down, and said again, "Kelsie, I am hungry." I said, "Rick, that is not my concern." I closed my eyes and then felt something hovering over me. I opened my eyes, and he began to strangle me as our daughter lay next to me on the bed. I fought him the best I could, but my sister, who had been spending some time at the house, overheard the struggle and entered our bedroom, causing him to stop. I hurled insults at him, hoping to hurt him emotionally because he had just hurt me, but he didn't stop trying to jump over my sister and my niece to come after me. My sister finally talked him into going downstairs while she stayed and asked me what had happened. I told her all that had transpired. She then went downstairs and asked him what had gone on. She was shocked because she thought that, after getting back together, we were doing well. Rather than show any remorse, he worked to defame my character. He told her about my relations with Lamar.

I remember feeling broken, listening to him, hoping to hear some remorse in his voice, but I never heard it. My daughter slept through the entire event. I still can't believe she slept through it all, but I was thankful that she did. I locked myself in our bedroom the entire night, trying to figure out a plan. I got myself and my daughter dressed and left, and that was the last night we spent in that house. I was finally done.

Oddly enough, it took all that for me to finally wake up. When I speak of waking up, I mean it was as if my mind and my actions finally came into alignment. I was ashamed of myself. How did I get myself so deeply involved with a man like that and go so far as to marry him? The first three weeks after walking out, I didn't have time to think about it; I needed to find a place for me and my daughter to live. I wanted to maintain as much stability as possible for her despite the circumstances. I spent my days working and being present for her, and my nights crying and searching for a place for us to live. God provided for me to have enough money for a security deposit and first month's rent. The obstacle was my credit, which was horrible. The marriage left me in a bad financial state. It's in these moments that we really are able to stand still and see God work in our lives. I was able to find a place in proximity to my daughter's preschool, affording me the ability to keep some things stable and consistent in her life. I didn't have much time to sit still and process all that had transpired; I had to just keep moving.

It's been four years since my divorce finalized, and I recently sat down with a therapist and began to process my life, not just my marriage. My divorce was the apex of all of my life experiences and a culmination of my decisions. The root of it all began way before Rick; it stemmed from a series of traumatic experiences that left me with deep feelings of rejection, embodied by so much fear. Those feelings were paralyzing. They were holding me back from living a life of joy and freedom.

Pastor A.R. Bernard often says, "We live life in levels and arrive in stages." Pain has been more real to me than happiness. I have functioned in the area of hardship more often than calmness. It makes sense that I would cling to what I know. Abuse in all of its forms had been ingrained in my past; despite my efforts to run from it, I ran directly to it because it is my predisposition. It was the area of my impairment; my movements were not voluntary, they were innate. The chaos of my marriage brought about this clarity. Some may argue that I could have gotten clarity without going through all that I did, and yes, it is possible. I often ask myself, *Would I have been at this level of understanding and clarity if I didn't?* I am still pondering the answer to that question.

Chapter 8

My First Love

If you return to me, I will restore you so you can continue to serve me. If you speak good words rather than worthless ones, you will be my spokesman. You must influence them; do not let them influence you! (Jeremiah 15:9, NLT)

I remember crying out to God one night when my emotions had overwhelmed me. I asked Him, "Why am I not loved? Why doesn't anyone love me?" He answered me as if He was crying out to me, saying, "You are loved. You are loved." It has been hard to believe those three words because love has always felt like it evaded me. I had no understanding of what it was. Also, I couldn't understand how others could love me, especially since I didn't know how to love myself.

In movies or TV shows, you often see a character smack another character in the face when they want to get their attention, or they simply tell them to "wake up." My "wake up" came in the form of someone strangling me. In one instant, my whole life changed. I was completely broken. There was the shame of admitting that I was that woman who was susceptible to abusive relationships. I had married the stereotypical abusive partner, yet I downplayed his actions for so long. I couldn't hide it anymore because my family knew about it. He didn't even have the restraint to attack me when my family was not in the house. He didn't even have the restraint to not do it while our child slept right beside me. He didn't have the restraint to stop and think that I was once his friend. We had known each other our entire adult life. He didn't love me enough to care.

I could no longer act as if I had my life together. I was forced to show my vulnerability in such a way that it was fully exposed.

The night Rick tried to strangle me was the last night we ever lived in a house together. I left the next morning and never looked back. Once I secured housing for me and my daughter, it was time to figure out what had brought me to that place and how to never go back here.

I began to seek God like never before. The pain was too great for me to handle, and when it came, I cried out to Him. Scripture says, *"In my desperation I prayed, and the LORD listened; he saved me from all my troubles"* (Psalm 34:6, NLT). As I prayed, I asked the Lord to show me what brought me to that point and help me to learn, heal, and never return to that place.

Pray Without Ceasing

I read about a woman once who had a desperate desire to have a child. She had love, but as much as she was loved, the one thing that would ease the burden of her heart was a child of her own. She was mocked and scrutinized for not being able to conceive. One day, the overwhelming pain of her unmet desire overtook her, and she cried out to the Lord in utter desperation and anguish. She couldn't even verbalize her request. With tears streaming down her face, her heart spoke to the Lord what her mouth could not. Then her answer came, in a package that was offensive to her flesh. This woman was Hannah, and her answer came in the package of Eli, who accused her of being drunk in the house of worship.

Hannah's story in the book of 1 Samuel teaches us that the deepest pain brings forth the purest prayer. If we would shut up long enough to let our heart speak to God, we would see our prayers answered faster. We often try to run away from the brokenness of our lives, not wanting to confront it, or we are so busy trying to cover it up that we do not take the time to adequately process it in order to heal.

God can't answer a convoluted prayer; well, actually, He can! But He won't. He won't because what good is your answered prayer if you have learned nothing from your brokenness? God does everything in such a way that we will have to seek Him to obtain understanding and insight. There is nothing that the omniscient and omnipotent God does not know or cannot do; so prayer is not a vehicle to get Him to move, but rather you! He already finished His work in you from the beginning, and then He rested because it was all good. He is simply waiting for you to arrive at His goodness for you.

Scripture says:

> Because the LORD had closed Hannah's womb, her rival kept provoking her in order to irritate her. This went on year after year. Whenever Hannah went up to the house of the LORD, her rival provoked her till she wept and would not eat (1 Samuel 1:6-7, NIV).

For years, Hannah dealt with the provocation from her rival, and she cried to the point that she would not eat. The question I have is *what was so different about this year?*

I believe she had finally had enough. She finally began to pray from a place of brokenness and humility, no longer driven by anger and frustration, but from a weakness that only God could give strength to. When she cried out this time to the Lord, she was humble and broken and no longer cared what others thought or what they had to say. She left pride at the door, got on her knees, and cried out in deep anguish, releasing all the built-up emotions and pain. It was then that Eli saw her.

Just let it out! God is not offended by your tears. Crying is not a sign of weakness; it is a way of release. Crying out is a form of surrender and admission to God, which simply says, *I can't do this on my own.* The psalmist said:

> The righteous cry out, and the LORD hears them; he delivers them from all their troubles. The LORD is close to the brokenhearted and saves those who are crushed in spirit (Psalm 34:17-18).

According to researchers, crying can benefit both your body and your mind. Crying detoxifies the body; it flushes stress hormones and other toxins out of your system. In addition, it helps you to self-soothe by activating the parasympathetic nervous system. This system helps your body rest and digest. Crying also causes you to release endorphins, also known as the feel-good chemicals, which can help you ease both physical and emotional pain.[1]

I spent a lot of time crying after the divorce. I spent six-plus years transforming into a wife and a mother, and then life shifted, and I had no idea how to shift with it. I had no idea who I was. My state was a person who lost her voice and her confidence, and any shred of worth she felt was gone. I cried out to the Lord, and He heard me and delivered me. I began asking God, "Who am I?"

He Is After Your Heart!

I mentioned earlier in the book that I was with someone for the entirety of my undergraduate studies. He was someone who befriended me during my freshman year of college, and then we became romantically involved. Our relationship followed the patterns of the previous relationships mentioned, but what makes it stand out is that it was the impetus that started it all. I was in a romantic relationship with him for

---

1. Ashley Marcin, Timothy J. Legg, PhD, "9 Ways Crying May Benefit Your Health," April 14, 2017, https://www.healthline.com/health/benefits-of-crying#self-soothing.

four years of my life, but he never gave me the title of "girlfriend." For years, we would have the same conversation over and over again, and he would never want to commit to me. It was the epitome of illusion. Year after year, I convinced myself that he would finally commit to me and call me his girlfriend. During our final year of undergrad, he finally gave me that elusive title—after four years! It was, however, short-lived. That was the year I graduated and went to Syracuse University for graduate school.

At the start of my first semester at Syracuse University, the conversation between he and I became very quarrelsome. One night, I prayed to the Lord a prayer that, in the years to come, I would use often, especially in reference to my relationships. I was in pain, and I cried out to the Lord for help. I had been so engulfed in the relationship that I had no idea how to leave it behind, despite how unhealthy and hurtful it had been. I asked the Lord to "do for me what I can't do for myself." I begged Him, if the relationship was not His plan for my life, to take it away. At three o'clock in the morning, I felt the need to check my email. I opened my inbox to find an email addressed from a girl I thought was his ex-girlfriend. She was extremely polite, and I could tell by the tone of her letter that she was probably feeling the same anguish I was. She explained to me that she had been in a relationship with Bailey since high school. Her intention was just to confirm whether or not we were seeing each other. I explained to her the complexities of our now five-year-old relationship. By the end of our email communication, it was clear to both of us that we had played the fool for years. We wished one another the best, and that was the end of our communication. I mustered up enough courage to call Bailey—not to argue, not to accuse him, but just to say goodbye. I had loved him for five years; I was naïve. He tried to apologize but respectfully allowed me to say goodbye without belaboring the conversation.

The pain from that breakup was like none other I had ever felt. I held on to the thought that God had something better for me. I would be good one instant, and in the next, I would break down and fall to my knees and cry out in anguish to God. One day, I was walking, and the Lord placed this scripture on my heart:

> "For I know the plans I have for you," declares the LORD, "plans to prosper you and not to harm you, plans to give you hope and a future. Then you will call on Me and come and pray to Me, and I will listen to you. You will seek Me and find Me when you seek Me with all your heart" (Jeremiah 29:11-13).

All your heart—those three words kept echoing in my mind. I said to the Lord, "But I *am* seeking You with all my heart." He then showed me that I wasn't, not as long as I kept allowing that relationship to get between Him and me. It was then that I began to seek God with an even deeper commitment. Before I even realized it, I had healed from the hurt of my breakup with Bailey.

In order to overcome something, you can't give it up and expect that the desire or attraction to it will just go away (in some cases it might, but I don't believe that's the way it generally works). You have to replace it with something else. I can only speak for myself, but after walking away from that situation, I began to spend a lot more time praying and reading the Bible. I focused my attention on growth in God, and it worked for me. Prayer never hurts, and it may not be the only thing you will do in your process of overcoming. After my divorce from Rick, I joined the YMCA and began to work out. I knew that I had to get out of the house or I would come home, curl up in a ball, and cry every night. I know I discussed how crying is beneficial, and it is, but everything in moderation. What I am trying to bring home is this: make God your priority, seek after what brings balance, and everything else will fall into place.

Stand on His Word!

Every year, my pastor announces a psalm for our church to recite and declare over our year. Over the years, I have made sure to read and recite this scripture almost daily, praying it over my life and my family. As I've put this into practice in my life, I have seen the promises of God's Scripture manifest in my life. The same is true in breaking unhealthy patterns; you must stand on God's Word. When faced with the uncertainty of a situation, the Word of God will be the lighthouse, as an indicator of safety ahead.

Psalm 23 is undoubtedly one of the most recited portions of Scripture. Anyone who has ever been exposed to church knows this psalm. Psalm 23 was what got me through my season of despair amidst a horrible divorce—the period in my life when I felt as if I had completely lost myself. The enemy did everything in his power to try to break me and cause me to lose my mind. I could have easily given in and conceded to defeat; it would have been more than understandable. Instead, I quoted this psalm in the morning, throughout the day, before bed, when I woke up in the middle of the night, and at any point I felt like giving up.

> The LORD is my shepherd; I shall not want. He makes me to lie down in green pastures; He leads me beside the still waters. He restores my soul; He leads me in the paths of righteousness for His name's sake. Yea, though I walk through the valley of the shadow of death, I will fear no evil; for you are with me; Your rod and Your staff, they comfort me. You prepare a table before me in the presence of my enemies; You anoint my head with oil; my cup runs over. Surely goodness and mercy shall follow me all the days of my life; and I will dwell in the house of the LORD forever (Psalm 23).

In the midst of one broken relationship after the next, you lose yourself. Over time, you question the person you are and if the words spoken by your abuser are true. My pattern was to be in abusive relationships, so my track record was filled with relationships and situations that pointed to what I believed was wrong with me.

At the end of my marriage, I had to believe that God had something better for me. Let me preface this by saying that I am not an advocate of divorce, but I do not believe that God's will for my life was to be continually abused and in harm's way. I take complete responsibility for my decision to marry my husband, knowing it was not God's will for my life. I know this because a week before my marriage, I had a vivid dream that showed me the abuse I would endure in this marriage. Instead of paying attention to the dream, I shrugged it off as just a bad dream. I also ignored the many times the Holy Spirit convicted me about the relationship throughout the years we were on the unhealthy rollercoaster.

I understood my disobedience in marrying my husband. However, once married, I did everything in my power to show honor to my husband and our marriage. I prayed and hoped that the circumstances of my marriage would change and that my husband would one day see me—see my heart. I prayed that he would allow me to love him and be able to see the marriage and the family we could have. Unfortunately, it did not appear that he could see it or that he even wanted to see it. I lived in fear and felt as if I was walking on eggshells for six and a half years.

There was nowhere left for me to go but up. I actually breathed a sigh of relief in the midst of my pain because I knew there were greater things in store for me. If there weren't, then that would make God a liar, and there is no chance that He is a liar!

I felt as if I had veered far away from His path and purpose for my life. It was as if I had wasted a large portion of time. I pondered on where I would have been had I not made some of the decisions I had made in the past. I was successful in so many areas in my life, but I felt like a continual failure in my relationships. I was determined to never lose time reenacting the same patterns. It was time to change! In order to change, I had to believe that it was possible for God to restore me. If He could restore me, then He could also redeem the time that was lost.

Hold firm to God's promises. I found comfort in knowing that God had better for me, and that He would work all things out for my good. He has better for you too!

> So I will restore to you the years that the swarming locust has eaten, the crawling locust, the consuming locust, and the chewing locust… You shall eat in plenty and be satisfied (Joel 2:25-26).

Chapter 9

Take Care of You

Stop Beating Yourself Up!

It was difficult writing about some of the events that transpired in my relationships. There were times in my process of writing that I didn't want to do it because I couldn't handle reliving some of the events that occurred. Whew, I really was a mess!

We all have messy stories—some more than others. The goal of this book is for you to be able to identify your patterns in the midst of each failed relationship. Once identified, begin the work to change them. It's easier said than done, but you can do it. In order to do this, you have to stop beating yourself up about your mistakes, no matter how small or large. It doesn't matter how scandalous or demeaning. Your mistakes were all building blocks for a better you.

> There is therefore now no condemnation to those who are in Christ Jesus, who do not walk according to the flesh, but according to the Spirit (Romans 8:1).

This is why your relationship with God is key. It is through this relationship that we gain knowledge of *self.* This relationship has to be the foundational relationship because any effort made apart from it will be deficient. Not understanding your purpose—the reason you were created—will always lead you to make decisions for your life that may feel good at first but will inevitably be destructive. In order to be effective in your future relationships, you will have to walk according to the Spirit.

Your mistakes were all building blocks for a better you.

What does it mean to walk according to the Spirit? I am simply saying to seek God before you make a move. No more impulsive behaviors; take time to analyze the situation and look at it from all angles. For what man builds a house without considering the cost? It is key, and I repeat key, to have a high level of standards. Standards are simply levels of quality or attainment. These, in their simplest form, are your boundaries.

Does this mean you will get it right all the time? Maybe, but the chances are you will mess up one or two times again. However, I guarantee that you will be more attuned to the signs of an unhealthy relationship and more perceptive to your own patterns. If you walk in the Spirit, there will be an uncomfortableness, and you will lack peace until your actions go in accordance to your purpose. I govern my life by Habakkuk 2:2-3:

> Then the LORD answered me and said: "Write the vision and make it plain on tablets, that he may run who reads it. For the vision is yet for an appointed time; but at the end it will speak, and it will not lie."

I love this scripture! Let's break down the steps:

1. Pray: "The LORD answered me and said." Closed mouths don't get fed. You have to put it before the Lord first.
2. Write It Down: "Write the vision and make it plan." Be intentional about what you want and how you want it.

3. Have Your Proof: "That he may run who reads it." Life doesn't just happen; we live on levels and arrive in stages. God takes us through various stages of life, and in the midst of these stages, there are levels that we must attain in order to move on to the next stage. This is typically the preparation stage. Everything you go through, between the time of writing the vision and seeing it come to fruition, is preparation. We prepare through the various levels that we attain.

4. Wait: "For the vision is yet for an appointed time." There is purpose in the waiting. It all has to align with God's purpose for your life. The reason we pray first is because we need to initiate godly alignment.

5. Let It Speak: "But at the end it will speak, and it will not lie." Your promise will speak for itself, and you will have no other choice but to acknowledge the sovereign hand of God.

There is purpose in the waiting.

The reason we arrive in stages is simply because we have to live, grow, and mature. I have yet to meet anyone who has never stumbled in life. In fact, I have learned that it is those who stumble the most and learn from it who will go on to do great things.

Recognizing your patterns is not a quick or immediate process. Until now, you have spent your entire life developing those patterns and functioning in them. It will take time to change, but with the help of the Holy Spirit, you will begin to see change.

> And we know that all things work together for good to those who love God, to those who are the called according to His purpose (Romans 8:28).

You are smarter and braver than you think. Your mistakes have made you the most qualified for functioning and developing highly effective and sustainable relationships. I say this because you already know how *not* to do it. This allows you to harness humility and wisdom and use them in your future relationships. This is very powerful as you walk in your purpose.

Confide in Someone!

> And they overcame him by the blood of the Lamb and by
> the word of their testimony (Revelation 12:11).

After my divorce, my church's biblical institute offered a small group called "Divorce Recovery." It was the first time that workshop was ever offered there. I am usually the kind of person who holds everything inside and doesn't say much to others about the deep things that are bothering me. I say that because, if you know me, you might think that I am an open book. I am not. I share surface-level things with others, but no one ever knows the deep things. These are the things that keep me awake at night—the things that, when I attempt to talk to God, the words can never be uttered in English—only the groaning and the utterance of the Spirit, as tears stream down my face. It was a big step for me to join that small group and be transparent about my marriage and what led to our divorce. However, I did it for the purpose of changing my pattern of always holding things in. God has to be invited into your pain, and He should be the first Person you run to. I have learned that God also uses the wisdom of others to help you overcome.

The Enemy wants you to hold everything in and keep it to yourself. This is the perfect opportunity for condemnation and defeating thoughts to enter. In order to overcome, you have to first trust in the redemptive blood of Christ and speak your truth. Share your testimony! There is nothing you have done in this life that someone else has not experienced. It is important to have an avenue to process your experiences so the healing can begin. This can be a small group or even a big group. It can also be a confidant or a therapist. Depending on the severity of the trauma, there may be a need for a trained professional.

The small group I joined gave me the opportunity to not only hear the stories of others but to speak out loud about a situation that was hurtful and humiliating to me. Remember, I had a huge issue with people seeing my vulnerability. It was my time to take off the mask. It was too hard trying to live up to the image of perfection I had created for myself. I don't know who I thought I was fooling.

Take off the mask! Let the healing begin—you deserve it!

Gratitude

There is a psychological term called *negative bias*. This theory basically states that we hold on to the wound of a rebuke more strongly than a good or positive experience. In a meeting with my therapist one day, I told her that I felt as if I was prone to negative friendships or people I know do not mean me well. I began to tell her the story of a friendship I had with one of my co-workers. I am not usually one to spend time with my colleagues outside of work, but this particular co-worker and I developed a friendship outside of the office. We would go to movies together, she would babysit my daughter at times, and she was someone that I often confided in. One day, she made a comment to me that hurt my feelings very much. Based on the comment she made, I determined that she was not a good friend, and I began to distance myself from her. I would no longer spend time with her outside of work. Despite my decision to discontinue the friendship, I found myself still drawn to being around her when we were at work, and although I no longer trusted her, I would still confide in her. It was a struggle in me because I determined within myself that she was not a friend, yet I would still let my guard down when talking with her.

As I discussed it with my therapist, I related it to a need for acceptance. My therapist, in turn, introduced the term *negative bias*. As we talked, I realized that from the time my co-worker made the hurtful comment to me, I interpreted all of her successive actions based on that one comment she had made. The more I discussed this with my therapist, the more I realized that my co-worker had also provided support to me at times when I didn't have anyone else. I had forgotten all of the positive aspects of our interactions because of one comment I chose to focus on. The dynamics with my co-worker had little to do with a need for acceptance, but more to do with the fact that I genuinely enjoyed her company. I was so offended by her comment that I refused to admit it, and I perceived her as an enemy. If I had only taken the time to just let her know that her comment hurt my feelings and given her the opportunity to explain her side, then two years of resentment might have been filled with a friendship of growth and maturity.

The point is that we focus too much on the negative. We give more life to the trauma of the past than the present and the joys that are in each day. *"But one thing I do, forgetting those things which are behind and reaching forward to those things which are ahead"* (Philippians 3:13).

A couple of months after my divorce, a friend invited me to join a private group she started on Facebook. It was a gratitude group. This group consisted of her closet friends, and every morning, each person would write the things they were grateful for in that day. In the beginning, it was difficult to write a lot, probably because I was newly divorced, broke, and exhausted all the time. However, I persevered and did this daily. I should mention that I was waking up every morning feeling extremely depressed and unhappy. I was functioning from day to day because I had a little girl who depended on me.

I gradually started seeing changes in my disposition, once I pushed myself to focus daily on what I was grateful for. I began to wake up at times feeling bursts of energy and joy. I literally started seeing how great I was, and I was so thankful for the opportunity to still be in the land of the living. My focus switched from the negative in my life to what was good about my life.

According to UCLA's Mindfulness Awareness Research Center, regularly expressing gratitude literally changes the molecular structure of the brain, keeps the gray matter functioning, and makes us healthier and happier.

Changing your mindset and your outlook on life is not going to happen overnight; it is constant and daily work. Think of it this way: you are undoing every negative thought, perception, and dialogue you've had with yourself since you were a child. It is consistent and persistent work, but you can do it!

Handle Your Stress

It's important to pursue interests that feed your soul. One of my interests is bird watching. I am by far not an expert, but a true novice. Slowly, as I pursued my interest in birds, I began to learn and recognize the different species of bird, paying attention to their uniqueness in appearance and also the variations in their bird calls. It has always been an interest of mine, but I allowed it to be dormant, not giving much attention to it for years.

My favorite bird is the eagle. I love this bird, not only for the biblical symbolism, but the more I read about the characteristics of an eagle, the more fascinated I become. One of the most interesting facts I found out about an eagle is that it can spot its prey from two miles away. I am sure this ability gives the eagle time to prep and strategize. Wouldn't it be amazing to have the ability to see your opponent from miles away? It would give you time to prepare and strategize in order to be victorious in every situation.

When you are under tremendous stress, it takes a toll on your emotional, physical, and spiritual health. Stress blocks your ability to see what is ahead, thereby leaving you unprepared and without a plan. Stress is a distraction from efficiency. This is why it is important to find a healthy way to handle your stress.

Here are a few important ways to handle your stress:

1. Cast Your Burden on the Lord

    - Cast your burden on the LORD, and He shall sustain you (Psalm 55:22).

- Casting all your care upon Him, for He cares for you (1 Peter 5:7).
- You have granted me life and favor, and Your care has preserved my spirit (Job 10:12).

God is waiting for you to surrender it all to Him. He wants to show you that He has it all under control. He knows this ends with you winning and Him getting the glory.

2. Speak Life

- Death and life are in the power of the tongue, and those who love it will eat its fruit (Proverbs 18:21).
- Even so the tongue is a little member and boasts great things. See how great a forest a little fire kindles! (James 3:5)
- The tongue of the wise uses knowledge rightly (Proverbs 15:2).

Your words shape your world. Speak words of hope and of wisdom. Speak about the end goal, not your obstacles.

3. Exercise

This is not a novel idea. Exercise relieves stress, and it makes you feel happy. Think about a good workout where your clothes are dripping from sweat. Think of every drop as a stress droplet dripping off of you. During exercise, your body releases chemicals that can improve your mood and make you feel more relaxed.

After my divorce, I was depressed, and I didn't want my daughter to see my depression. I made sure we were staying busy. The local YMCA became our go-to stop for activities. Working out helped me to release tension and anxiety. I started out slowly because it had been three years since I had formally worked out. I took a "WERQ" class with Kelly K., who was an extremely energetic instructor with a love for twerking. I would step into that class, start moving to the beat of the music, and just go for it. I am a highly uncoordinated person, so you can imagine what I probably looked like in that class. However, it made me feel sexy and free. This was important because my self-esteem had been extremely compromised throughout my marriage. In this dance class, I felt sexy and attractive again, all while getting physically fit.

Take Inventory

As you've been reading this book, you have probably identified certain relationships in your life that are unhealthy. In my case, it wasn't only the relationship with my husband that was toxic. And there were other relationships that were not toxic but needed clear and defined boundaries. I have come to learn that people only treat you how you allow them to treat you.

The hardest challenge in getting over the pain of my divorce was not understanding how my husband could treat me with such hatred and disdain. The verbal abuse continued long after our separation and divorce. I remember sitting in the waiting room of the family courtroom, and Rick walked in. He tried to start up a conversation with me, but I ignored him. He was very persistent, but once he realized that I was not entertaining it, he started in. Rick began to insult and berate me. I sat there with a flat affect, not knowing how to react. My only reaction was to look him up and down and then laugh as if he was a joke.

Inside, I had had enough. Despite everything that had happened, I still worked hard to maintain as civil a relationship as possible for the sake of our daughter. At the time, I was under a lot of stress at work, searching for a new home, and busting my butt to barely make ends meet. That day in court, I reached the edge of what I could take. I went into a depressive and frustrated mode for a couple of months afterward. It bothered me so much that he thought he had the right to speak to me that way. It bothered me that I allowed him to do it. I struggled with the desire to curse him out; nothing I would say would be in line with my Christian values. I maintained my composure because I knew that got under his skin more. Most importantly, I held it together because I don't want my daughter to grow up with two parents who constantly argue. A big part of it is that I believe God's vengeance is so much better than anything I could ever say or do.

For a couple of months, the frustration of his behavior continued to bother me. It was less about him and more about me. I had to realize that I had given him permission, time and time again, to be disrespectful to me. I also realized that I don't defend myself often enough. Scripture says that we are to turn the other cheek, but I think we often misunderstand what is meant by turning the other cheek. You are no one's doormat or punching bag. It is imperative that you set your boundaries with people and help them to understand what you are willing to take and what you are not.

One day, Rick made me so angry that I finally gave it to him. I called out his manipulative ways and spoke to his attempts of intimidation. I informed him that he would never again speak to me the way he had. I also informed him that if he continued, I would file an order of protection against him and utilize two years of documented email and texting threads filled with his threats and insults to prove the history of his behavior. I can emphatically say that, since that day, he has yet to disrespect me.

Take an inventory of all the toxic and unhealthy relationships in your life. You will know which ones they are because they're the ones that give you the most stress and bring about the most anxiety. After my divorce, I also distanced myself from certain family members. The distancing may be for a short period of time, or it may be for a long period of time. Whatever you need to do, do it.

Let's be clear that I am not talking about isolation, but stepping away from certain unhealthy situations in order to take time and evaluate what created the unhealthy dynamics. Once you are able to recognize the root of it, it's time to make a decision as to what you plan to do about it. My issue was simply that I let people walk all over me. I used forgiveness as a way to excuse my tolerance for the bad behavior of others. That was wrong in so many ways; it can develop a pattern of people taking from you without anyone giving back or pouring back into you. In the end, you are left beat down and completely drained. Stop it!

It is imperative for you to know your worth. When you know your worth, you are a better judge of what you deserve. This is the key factor that will not only attract, but also repel, certain people in your life. Do you want to know the real reason you kept getting into a relationship with the same person in different bodies? It is because you are still the same person. You allow them to treat you based on your valuation of yourself. As soon as you raise your standards to meet what you are worth, you will begin to attract the right people into your life. This is not to say that the wrong people will not come, but with the right self-worth, you won't even entertain them. Remember, even Jesus had crazy people following Him, but each time they tried something, He just rebuked them.

Set Your Goals

One of my favorite movies is called *Finding Forrester*. This movie is about an inner-city high school youth who lives in the Bronx. This young man is a genius but hides it because where he is from, it's not popular to be smart. Instead, he masks his intelligence by playing basketball and getting good enough grades that keep him in a safe zone so no one finds out his secret. Then, one day, he meets a mysterious man who lives in one of the apartment buildings in his neighborhood. The man turns out to be one of the greatest writers in the world: William Forrester. The world thinks he is dead, but instead, he has been hiding out in his apartment for years, afraid to venture out because of agoraphobia. Agoraphobia, in its simplest form, is the fear of crowds. These two unlikely characters form a friendship and a bond that causes both to venture out of their comfort zones and finally show the world who they really are. The young man is then launched into greatness because of that encounter and friendship.

My point in saying all of this is that relationships have the ability to launch you into greatness or utter defeat. That's why who you surround yourself with is so important. There are three relationships that will be the most important in your life: your relationship with God, your relationship with yourself, and your relationship with others—in that exact order.

> But seek first the kingdom of God and His righteousness,
> and all these things shall be added to you (Matthew 6:33).

The order has to be right. I can't love myself, or even know how to love myself, if I don't seek my Creator to understand who I am. I can't learn to trust Him if I don't make an active effort to seek Him. It is through seeking God that I will get to know myself in Him. If I have no understanding of myself, I cannot fully love myself. If I do not love myself, I cannot love others. Without these three factors working symbiotically, I will never reach my potential.

This is why the Enemy has attacked you so fiercely in your relationships; it's because he is after your potential. The first time I saw the movie *Finding Forrester,* something was stirred on the inside of me. I was fifteen years old, and I had never experienced that insane feeling of passion for something. I remember thinking that I wanted to be like William Forrester; I wanted to write books that people would talk about and discuss long after I leave this earth. I have no idea how I will accomplish this, but I began to work with what I had. I followed the leading of the Lord to write about my past experiences and what I learned from them. I don't know where it will lead or if it will lead to anything at all, but I am not willing to find out what will happen if I don't follow the leading of the Lord.

There are things that God has put in your heart to accomplish. If you are unsure of what they are, think back to the last time you felt an overwhelming desire or passion to do something or to be a part of something. It may just be that you have yet to discover it, but seek God for wisdom about it.

Set your goals! The eagle is able to see its prey from miles away. You have to be able to see your future from where you are now. This will create your focus; your focus will be driven by your faith; your faith will develop your discipline; and your discipline will cement your ability to accomplish it.

I know what you're thinking: *I thought this was a book about relationships.* It is. You are most attractive when you are working. If you study some of the women in the Bible, you will notice a common theme: they worked! For example:

Rebekah

Rebekah came out with her jar on her shoulder. She was the daughter of Bethuel son of Milkah, who was the wife of Abraham's brother Nahor. The woman was very beautiful, and a virgin; no man had ever slept with her. She went down to the spring, filled her jar and came up again. The servant hurried (Genesis 24:15-17, NIV).

Ruth

So she went out, entered a field and began to glean behind the harvesters. As it turned out, she was working in a field belonging to Boaz, who was from the clan of Elimelek. Just then Boaz arrived from Bethlehem and greeted the harvesters, "The LORD be with you!" "The Lord bless you!" They answered. Boaz asked the overseer of his harvesters, "Who does that young woman belong to?" (Ruth 2:3-5, NIV)

The Virtuous Woman

> She seeks wool and flax, and willingly works with her hands. She is like the merchant ships, she brings her food from afar. She also rises while it is yet night, and provides food for her household, and a portion for her maidservants. She considers a field and buys it; from her profits she plans a vineyard (Proverbs 31:13-18).

In the stories of both Rebekah and Ruth, their work placed them in the right place at the right time. In both illustrations, as they worked, they were noticed. The virtuous woman is a depiction of what happens after marriage, but we can ascertain that marriage didn't make her the businesswoman she was; she already possessed the skills and was working with them before she married.

Write the vision and make it plain, according to Habakkuk 2. Set your goals that will propel you to the vision God has given you. If you do not know the vision for your life, simply ask God to show you and give you wisdom. As you write them and put them in front of you, watch how God's grace abounds to bring them to fruition!

Chapter 10

The Shift

*In him we were also chosen, having been predestined accord-
ing to the plan of him who works out everything in conformity
with the purpose of his will (Ephesians 1:11, NIV).*

I began writing this book almost thirteen years ago. All I knew at that time was that my journey down this path needed to be told, and if my story helped someone else, then none of it was in vain. It bothers me the way women are viewed and characterized when they play the cards they've been dealt. My reason for saying this is simply to eliminate the notion of "damaged goods." To eliminate the notions of the promiscuous woman and the judgments against the single mother of three, all with different fathers. I also want to eliminate the comparisons of what constitutes a good woman as opposed to the one who is considered damaged goods or, a term I recently heard, *washed up.* I would rather introduce two types of women to the world: the broken and the healed.

The word *broken* referrs to a physical or emotional disintegration. What once was whole is now shattered, fragmented pieces of a person. The broken woman is not kept or honored. Instead, her actions are looked upon as promiscuous and not respectful. I have often said that there is no such thing as a woman who just loves to sleep with multiple men. I will continue to say it because I believe it strongly. To be clear, when I say multiple partners, I am talking about an unhealthy number of men within a short and/or sometimes overlapping timeframe. God did not build us this way. The act of sex was designed in such a way that the male has the ability to enter and also to leave a deposit. However, this is not so for women, and the roles cannot in any way be switched. I would argue that when a woman chooses to engage in having multiple sexual partners, there is a deeper desire there to be filled. There is a deposit that they are looking for or a deeper need to be met. This does not overlook the man who engages with multiple sexual partners as defined above. I would say that the man has deeper issues to address as well, but my opinion is based on my womanly perspective and experience. The reason a woman engages in certain relational behaviors has a deeper meaning. Her relational patterns have a story behind them.

At this stage of my life, I consider myself on the journey of being healed. It has been over four years since my divorce, and I attempted to date a couple of guys. They didn't quite work out but helped me along my healing journey.

The first guy is the one I call the "eye opener." One night, as I was going into church, Jim held the door open for me. I remember looking at him and thinking he was a nice-looking guy. This was the first time I allowed myself to notice him. On another occasion, as we were leaving church, he struck up a conversation with me as I walked to my car. He politely held the door open for me and asked if we could exchange numbers. I agreed, and we exchanged numbers. Just after he took my phone number, as I sat in the car and he was about to close my door, he said, "I have eight kids." I naturally yelled in shock, "Eight kids?" He said yes, and I said okay. I began to rationalize in my mind that everyone has a past, and I should still give him a chance. I ended up going on a date with him. There was a creek walk not too far from my house, and on nice days people were out walking and enjoying the outdoors. I like walking as a first date because you have nothing to do but walk and talk. It's one of those dates in which you find out a lot about the other person, and boy, did I find out a lot about him! I tried to keep an open mind, but the best way to put it is that he had a very colorful past. In a nutshell, he told me he had tendencies to be verbally abusive and had, in his youth, been physically violent toward his significant other, but not anymore.

You'd think I would have gone running in the other direction, but I didn't. We then went out to eat dinner at a moderately inexpensive restaurant. We had some interesting conversation and, as it came time to pay the check, he made jokes about hoping his credit card would not get declined. I had not eaten all my food, so he asked me if he could have the remainder to take home to his son; I humbly obliged. Still, I did not run. We continued to talk for a week or two, and then he ghosted me. *He* ghosted *me.* In hindsight, I realized that I had become incredibly clingy and needy. The clinginess and neediness came from the fear of being alone, so any attention that took that feeling away would do. I remember hanging out with a friend of mine, and I was telling her about how he ghosted me. She was familiar with the whole story. As we were talking, she asked, "How low can your self-esteem be? That's so desperate." She was a very blunt and straightforward person and still is to this day. Those words pierced me and devastated me at the same time. She was right; I was desperate. It was then that my eyes opened. I saw for the first time the level of brokenness that was in me. It was embarrassing and, at the same time, revealing. That moment brought me to another level in my understanding of my worth. I didn't realize how low my self-concept was. I was willing to step back into the same situation all over again, just to have the ability to say I had someone.

I continued to seek God throughout all of this and prayed that He would help me to never repeat the unhealthy patterns that were so engrained in me. I began to write a list of qualities I wanted in a man; some were a wish list, and others were must-haves. Another thing I did was create a vision board. The vision board helped me to pay attention to the changes I wanted to make in my life. My vision board consisted of goals that would help me find peace and happiness in my life. Also on the vison board was that I wanted to buy a house. I was nowhere near being able to purchase a home, but I determined within myself, after needing to stay in the home of close friends after my marriage ended, that I would make sure my daughter and I would never have to worry about that again.

That's where Ash came in. I had known Ash for years; in fact, he was my landlord the year I got married. At the time, Ash was also married with children. He was a nice person, but I didn't care for him much as a landlord because he once was accusatory toward me when the kitchen sink in my apartment was blocked up. He gave me a look that insinuated I caused the blockage, which ended up being caused by the college students upstairs. They were throwing coffee grounds into the sink, which inevitably caused the blockage. Needless to say, it was interesting to me when the attraction came about. I would see Ash at church, but we would say hello and keep it moving. Ash began to go slightly out of his way to say hello to me. One day, I asked myself if Ash was giving me a vibe. I then brushed it off because I was too annoyed with men at that point. One day, Ash saw me at church and, once again, went out of his way to say hello. I waved at him in an almost dismissive way. It was then the Lord spoke to me, "Do not close doors that I have opened for you." I said to the Lord in disbelief, "Who, Ash?" Nevertheless, I was intrigued. Ash was a financial advisor, and he had been teaching financial classes at our church's Bible institute. One day, I reached out to him and asked if he could help me get my finances in order so I could eventually get a house. He willingly did. We sat down, and I had to tell him all the tawdry details about my finances. He was extremely helpful, and he made owning a house seem like an easily attainable thing, whereas I saw it as a huge mountain.

Not too long after sitting down and talking with Ash, he invited me and my friend to an event. Until that event, I did not see Ash as someone I would date. He just didn't seem like my type. However, that night, I saw him differently. I blamed it on the one glass of wine I drank, but I was very touchy feely, clingy, and just way too much that night. Oddly enough, that did not completely turn him off. I thought that our personalities would be too different because I had only known him as being a serious finance guy, but he was actually funny and sarcastic, which I enjoyed.

Ash and I went out the following Monday to the creek to walk! That conversation was much different. I don't know if it was the nine-year difference between Ash and I, but he spoke into my life with such wisdom that night. I opened up to him in ways I had never opened up to anyone. We talked about my frustration at work, the divorce, the past, and so much more. He poured into me such good advice. We talked so much that the sun went down, and there we were on our walk; it was pitch dark. That was not romantic at all because the animal sounds were getting louder. We eventually made it back to our cars and went our separate ways, but he called me, and we talked until almost three o'clock in the morning. In the midst of the conversation, Ash brought up my behavior at the event and how strong I came on to him. He didn't do it in a way that shamed me but called out the inappropriateness of it. I can't explain it, but it was done in such a regal way.

Ash and I had a great week and spent all of our time together. We were both kid-free that week, and we took complete advantage of it. However, at the close of the week, I had a serious conversation with Ash and told him I didn't think he was healed from his divorce. Despite the fact that he had been divorced for three years, he still had a lot of healing to do. Ash and I would meet for lunch at different times, but he eventually became so consumed in work and life that things between us changed. It was apparent that we were at different phases in life. I didn't want to let go of him, but life has a way of making those decisions for us. We check in on each other from time to time, but I never again had time with him like that one week. I took Ash's advice as it pertained to work, finances, and even the hard conversations, and within a year, I purchased my first home. In addition, I finally advocated for myself at work. The confidence I obtained from advocating for myself at work eventually led to me owning my worth as an employee. A year later, I started my own consulting agency. It was as if a shift had happened in my life. I will always appreciate the time I spent with him. It was good to experience a man pour into me, rather than just take from me. It was not all perfect with Ash, but for the first time in my life since high school, I had an actual interaction with the opposite sex that wasn't toxic.

* * *

It has been three years since that time, and I am still single. That's not to say there haven't been men who've approached me and wanted to talk, but I am at a place these days where I understand my worth and what I want out of a relationship. I no longer function from a place of deficit or, better said, desperation. In these three years of being single, I spent more alone time with God; and, in getting to know Him, I got to know me.

In my relationships, I no longer function from a place of rejection—the rejection that caused me to live in fear of not being wanted or people walking away from me. This took God, a therapist, and time. The more I became free from the bondage of the fear of rejection, the more I began to dominate in life. I became a *boss!* I began functioning from a place of adequacy, as in who I am is enough. I am enough as a mother, as a daughter, as a friend, as a woman, and any other hat in my life that I currently wear and will eventually wear. I am a better mother because I no longer live in fear of being a bad mother. I no longer seek to change myself to accommodate the relationships in my life; I acknowledge my gifts and flaws, and I appreciate those who accept all the best and worst parts of me. I began selecting jobs based on work that drives my passion and compliments my gifts and talents. I don't stay where I am tolerated but, rather, among those who celebrate me. I feel whole! Wholeness is not the absence of mistakes or bad days, but the acceptance of every day. It is the mindset in which I accept every good thing and every bad thing, but in contentment and anticipation of the good. The good is God's definition of good, and not of evil, but to get me to an expected end. When the bad comes, I no longer think of it as being on account of a deficit in me.

Brokenness, in God's eyes, is being so crushed by the sin and darkness of the world that we recognize there is no place to turn but to God.

I tell these two contrasting stories to display growth. It wasn't pretty because I was still a mess of a person. My sense of worth, self-esteem, and image were low. Growth is continuous, not instantaneous, and it requires doing the work from the inside out. I have gotten to a place where I can want a relationship and still be okay in the waiting. I now know and appreciate myself outside of a relationship. I have found contentment in myself and recognize the beauty of God's creative work in me. It is no longer an act or me playing out the role of who I think I should be; it's simply me. I am created in His image, in His love, and in His wisdom.

Chapter 11

Go After Boaz!

*Praise be to the LORD, who this day has not left you without a
guardian-redeemer. May he become famous throughout Israel!
He will renew your life and sustain you in your old age. For
your daughter-in-law, who loves you and who is better to you
than seven sons, has given him birth (Ruth 4:14-15, NIV).*

I am almost certain that the majority of people who read the title of this
chapter thought this section would be about how to get a man—your
Boaz. I am so tired of hearing people talk about finding their Boaz. I
guarantee that by the end of this chapter, you will still want to go after
Boaz, but Boaz might have a significantly different appeal.

In the book of Ruth, Boaz is referred to as a "guardian-redeemer."
Guardian-redeemer was the legal term in those days for one who has the
obligation to redeem a relative in serious difficulty. For so many years,
when I read the book of Ruth, my understanding was that Ruth's loyalty
to Naomi inevitably led to her meeting Boaz. Boaz was the man who
treated her respectfully and kindly. In addition, he went after her; he did
what he could to get the girl. I am now convinced that Boaz was given
to Ruth as a reward for her faithfulness, but he wasn't the purpose. The
purpose was in what she birthed on account of being in relationship with

Boaz. Ruth was the mother of Obed, the father of Jesse, who was the father to David—the same bloodline as Jesus. I became so caught up in this romantic Bible story that I missed the whole point of the book, which was to preserve the bloodline of Jesus. We minimize the story of Ruth when we end the story at her finding Boaz.

You minimize your story when your end goal is only to find Boaz. The end goal should always be to understand why God has placed you on this earth and dominate in it. There is so much in you, and if you don't learn to cultivate your gifts in the seasons when you are alone, they will become diluted in the seasons when you are not. What are you here to do? If you don't know the answer, then it is time you start asking God. Purpose brings about direction, and without direction, you wander aimlessly. Figure out what you were placed here to do!

We have a tendency to prioritize the bridge over the destination.

We have a tendency to prioritize the bridge over the destination. The bridge is designed to help us get to our destination. The bridge symbolizes everything from where you started to where you will end up. It is important, but if you never reach your destination, would it have been worth it? The point I am trying to bring home is that once you find Boaz, he should display the qualities identified in this book, but it's not where your story ends. Your story is just beginning; you are on a journey to understand yourself—better yet, your "self" in God.

Go after Boaz! Boaz in the Bible is a *type* of Christ, meaning his character was symbolic of Christ the Redeemer. When Boaz is introduced, he immediately took notice of Ruth and showered her with favor. He showed Ruth kindness and gentleness, and made sure she was provided for. When the time was right, he stepped in to redeem her. Doesn't this remind you of Christ's love for us?

When you master the First Man, being in relationship with the next one will be so much more meaningful. The reason for this is that you are no longer operating from a place of deficiency or lack. The tragedies you call your past relationships failed because you had no idea who you were.

> Come, see a Man who told me all things that I ever did (John 4:29).

This is how you begin to break the patterns. When you recognize your worth (your kingdom worth), the possibilities are endless. You have been trying to get to your destination without a proper road map. It was never about finding Boaz; it is about God's kingdom. Boaz might be the bridge, but he is not the destination.

Break the hold that your past has on your life. For too long, you've allowed the trauma of your past to provide direction for your life. It has taken root and developed patterns that are unhealthy and unproductive. Continuous relationship failures have made you fearful; so fearful, in fact, that you have managed to keep everyone in your life at a safe distance—including God. But He wants more. He predestined you for something great. Some relationships were just distractions to deter you from your greatness. Other relationships were a setup to propel you toward your future, but because you were so fearful and built up such defenses, they never matured into what they were intended to be. The way to eliminate the fear is simply to receive God's love.

> There is no fear in love; but perfect love casts out fear, because fear involves torment (1 John 4:18).

Your first love is waiting for you. He is waiting for you to surrender it all to Him, so He can take it over. These were not the plans He had for you. This torment of continuous bad relationships was not His intention for you. As you begin this new journey, He is your companion. As you seek Him, He will guide the way. He is ready to unfold the beauty of love and all its magnitudes. Your life will never be the same again.

Changing Direction:

Breaking Unhealthy Relationship Patterns

An Interactive Workbook

Session 1: The Root of It All

Objective:

- Identify the different types of relationships

- Identify healthy vs. unhealthy relationships

- Identify your views of relationships and how your views affect how you relate to others

- Identify the origins of your relationship patterns

Common Types of Human Relationships

Under the various types of relationships below, list the people in your life that fall under those particular categories.

Romantic

____

____

____

Family

____

____

____

Work

Spiritual

Self

Healthy vs. Unhealthy Relationships

Healthy Characteristics

Unhealthy Characteristics

____

____

____

____

____

Activity #1: Memories

- List three of your earliest, most significant memories.

____

____

____

- When you think of these memories:

    o What emotions do you feel?

    o What thoughts or words come to mind?

    o What are your reactions (physical/emotional)?

____

____

____

____

____

How have these past experiences shaped your understanding of human relationships and interactions?

____

____

____

____

____

____

My earliest and most significant memories are:

____

____

____

____

____

____

____

The thoughts, words, reactions (physical/emotional) that come to mind:

____

____

____

____

____

____

____

____

Session 2: Scripts and Schemas

Objective:

- Understand what are cognitive scripts and schemas
- Identify various schemas in your life

Important Definitions:

Cognitive Script: The way you structure or organize your thoughts after multiple exposeures to the same or similar experiences.

Schema: Your way of thinking that aids you in structuring and making sense of information.

Person Schema: Our expectations about other people.

Self-Schema: Generalization about self from past experiences.

Social (Role) Schema: Behaviors expected in a social situation.

Event Schema: Scripts about expectations in social institutions.

Activity #2: Cognitive Script

My Cognitive Script (my understanding of relationships based on repeated experiences from my past and how I function in them):

____

____

____

Activity #3: Schemas

- Identify your schemas as they pertain to
  - Person Schema
  - Social (Role) Schema
  - Self-Schema
  - Event Schema

Person Schema—Our Expectations of Other People

What are my expectations of those I am in a relationship with?

Family:

____

____

____

Friends:

____

____

____

Significant Other:

____

____

____

Coworker:

____

____

____

Self:

____

____

____

Self-Schema: Generalization about self from past experience

How do I think others view me?

Self (How do I view myself):

____

____

____

Family:

____

____

____

Friends:

____

____

____

Significant Other:

____

____

____

Coworker:

____

____

____

Social (Role) Schema: Behaviors expected in a social situation

How do I treat them? How do I expect them to treat me? How do they actually treat me?

Family:

____

____

____

Friends:

____

____

____

Significant Other:

____

____

____

Coworker:

____

____

____

Event Schema: Scripts about expectations in social institutions (work, school, church, etc.)

How should I act in these settings? How do I actually act?

Work

____

____

____

____

Church

____

____

____

____

Marketplace (stores, etc.)

____

____

____

____

School (if applicable)

____

____

____

____

Other public areas

____

____

____

____

Session 3: Broken Record

Objective:

- Identification of the patterns in your relationships
- Mapping your relationship patterns: root, trauma, fear
- Relating your past experiences to your present relationship patterns

Patterns

Pattern: A repetitious, consistent sequence of behavior that manifests itself the same way every time.

Patterns are inherently rooted in your past!

- *They are reliable.*
- *They are safe.*
- *They are your go-to reaction.*
- *They are your defense.*

Activity #1: Your Patterns

Think back to the last three relationships that ended (either friendship, romantic, family, work, etc.)

- How did it start, what happened in the middle, what happened in the end?
- Were there any similarities?

Relationship #1

- How did it start?
- What happened in the middle?
- How did it end?

____

____

____

____

____

____

____

Relationship #2

- How did it start?
- What happened in the middle?
- How did it end?

____

____

____

____

____

____

Relationship #3

- How did it start?
- What happened in the middle?
- How did it end?

____

____

____

____

____

____

____

Similarities

List the similarities between those relationships:

____

____

____

____

____

____

Activity #2

- What are some noticeable fears when it comes to your relationships?
- Do these fears cause you to work harder at your relationships or cause you to want to run away (fight or flight)?
- Have your fears ever caused you to miss out on opportunities?

Session 4: Image Matters

Objective:

- Understand what is an image
- Identify your personal image and how it affects your relationships
- Develop a healthy self-image

Important Definitions:

Image: A depiction or likeness of a person or object.

Activity #1: Self Schema: Generalization about self from past experience

How do I view myself?

____

____

____

How do I feel others view me?

____

____

____

How do I want to be viewed?

____

____

____

What would it take for others to view me as I want to be viewed? How did I form my image?

____

____

____

Activity #2: Picture This!

In the space below, draw a self-portrait of yourself.

- How would you describe yourself based on your self-portrait?

- What do you feel is most important thing that others should know about you?

- Is there anything you want to change?

- How would you go about making that change?

Has your self-image ever affected any of your relationships (friendship, romantic, work, family)?
- What happened?
- What was the outcome?

Activity #3: Developing a Healthy Self-Image

What are three things you like about yourself?

1. ____

2. ____

3. ____

What are three things you can do to develop a more positive self-image?

1. ____

2. ____

3. ____

What are three challenges to developing a positive self-image?

1. ____

2. ____

3. ____

Session 5: Understanding Your Triggers

Objective:

- Understand what triggers are
- Identify defenses, guards, and walls you built to protect yourself.
- Understand why they exist and how your image plays a role
- Understand how your triggers affect your relationships
- Identify techniques to desensitize your trigger(s)

Important Terms:

Trigger: To cause an alarm to go off inside of you; a bomb exploding. ***A triggering event can cause an individual to revert to old ways or unhealthy patterns!***

- Something that re-triggers a past experience
- Incident that causes upsetting feelings
- Problematic behaviors that are often associated with a past trauma

Activity #1

Utilizing Section 1: The Root of It All, Activity 1: Memories, think back on one of the three significant memories and what emotions you feel when you think about this memory.

- Has there ever been a time when something someone did or said make you think back to this memory? There can also be other external stimuli that cause you to recall this memory, such as a smell, a TV show, a song.

- How do you typically feel in these moments?

- How do you typically react when this occurs?

- Has this reaction ever affected any of your relationships (friendship, romantic, family, work)?

Triggers

- The event triggers a fear.
- It tears at the fortified structures (or walls) you have built to protect yourself or keep unwanted things out.
- The response is usually an inherent pattern, thereby resulting in the same outcome. Your response is your defense.
- Unhealthy behavior patterns surface when there is an issue that has not been dealt with in your life.

Every pattern has a root, every root has a trauma, and every trauma opens the door to fear. Your fears will always paralyze your ability to move forward.

Understanding Your Triggers

Activity #2

- Do you see a pattern in your reactions to this event?

____

____

____

- Why do you think you react this way?

____

____

____

- Is there something you fear?

____

____

____

- Is there something you are trying to avoid with this reaction? If so, what is it? Why are you trying to avoid it?

____

____

____

____

Activity #3

What would happen if you no longer reacted to that memory in the same way anymore?

Previous Thought or Reaction:

____

____

____

____

____

New Thought or Reaction:

____

____

____

____

____

____

Session 6: Chaos in Clarity

Objective:

- Identify decisions that yielded either a positive or negative result
- Identify lessons learned in past experiences
- Identify new strategies that yield more positive results

Finding Clarity in Chaos

Activity #1

Think of a really chaotic time in your past.

- While you were going through this circumstance, what were your feelings?
- What decisions did you have to make in this circumstance? Did your decisions yield negative or positive results? What were they?
- What did you learn from going through this?

____

____

____

____

____

____

Activity #2

In hindsight:
- What did this chaotic event teach you about life?

____

____

____

- Did it bring clarity to anything?

____

____

____

- Have you been able to utilize what you have learned from that circumstance to make more positive decisions or to use it to help others?

____

____

____

- Did this circumstance bring clarity to any aspect of your life?

____

____

____

Session 7: Taking Care of You

Objective:

- Develop new patterns
- Identify a self-care routine
- Practice gratitude; change your outlook on life

Activity #1

What do you deserve out of life? Make a list of these things. *(This is not a list of wants but what you feel you deserve, which might be the same things.)*

- What are the things you want but are not on your list of things you deserve? If so, why don't you deserve these things?

____

____

____

____

- What keeps you from getting the things you want and also the things you deserve?

____

____

____

____

In order to change the patterns of life, you must first believe that you are deserving of good—that you are deserving of the good things, the good relationships, and having a good life. Until you come to this revelation, any attempts to change your patterns will be futile.

As he thinketh in his heart, so is he (Proverbs 23:7, KJV).

Activity #2: Goal Setting

- Write out your goals—both short-term and long-term goals.
- Writing out your goals creates a roadmap for your life. What is your plan to get there?
- Some like to say "Be realistic," I prefer to say "Be practical." Some of the greatest accomplishments came from those who dared to dream big!

WRITE IT DOWN!

What are your goals?

Goal 1:

____

____

____

My Plan:

____

____

____

* * *

Goal 2:

____

____

____

My Plan:

____

____

____

* * *

Goal 3:

____

____

____

My Plan:

____

____

____

* * *

Goal 4:

____

____

____

My Plan:

____

____

____

* * *

Goal 5:

____

____

____

My Plan:

____

____

____

* * *

Goal 6:

____

____

____

My Plan:

____

____

____

* * *

Tip 2: Gratitude

- Take time each day to write out what you are grateful for. It can be one thing or twenty things.
- Gratitude helps take the focus off of the negatives of life and focus on the good. This rewires your brain and you will begin to see the change in your outlook of life

Activity #3

Write three statements of gratitude:

1. ____

2. ____

3. ____

Activity #4: Self-Care

- What are some self-care routines that you do?

____

____

- How can you incorporate these routines regularly in your life?

____

____

- What are things you love to do, things that bring you joy?

____

____

- How can you do these things more often?

____

____

About the Author

Kelsie Harris-Knight is a native of Guyana, South America and came to the United States of America at the age of seven. She graduated with her Masters of Social Work from Syracuse University in 2005 and has worked over twenty years in the behavior health and human services field. Mrs. Harris-Knight spent many of those years working with families and youth helping them build healthy life skills and move beyond the trauma of their past to a more thriving life. Her work, professionally and personally, has been centered on helping others become their best self. She is passionate about helping people get to the core of life issues, understand them, and build healthy habits and skills to overcome them.

Kelsie can be reached at k.s.harrisknight@gmail.com.